Scary Stories
TREASURY

THREE BOOKS TO CHILL YOUR BONES

COLLECTED FROM FOLKLORE AND RETOLD
BY ALVIN SCHWARTZ

ILLUSTRATED BY STEPHEN GAMMELL

HarperCollins*Publishers*

Printed in the United States of America. For information address HarperCollins Children's Books, a division of HarperCollins Publishers, 1350 Avenue of the Americas, New York, NY 10019. www.harperchildrens.com

ISBN 0-06-026341-5

CONTENTS

Scary Stories to Tell in the Dark

Collected from American Folklore by

Alvin Schwartz

with drawings by Stephen Gammell

HarperCollins*Publishers*

 Printed in the United States of America. For information address HarperCollins Children's Books, a division of HarperCollins Publishers, 1350 Avenue of the Americas, New York, NY 10019.

Library of Congress Cataloging-in-Publication Data
Schwartz, Alvin.
Scary stories to tell in the dark.
Summary: Stories of ghosts and witches, "jump" stories, scary songs, and modern-day scary stories.
ISBN 0-397-31926-6 — ISBN 0-397-31927-4 (lib. bdg.)
ISBN 0-06-440170-7 (pbk.)
1. Ghost stories, American. 2. Tales, American. [1. Ghost stories. 2. Folklore—United States] I. Gammell, Stephen. II. Title.
PZ8.1.S399Sc 1981 80-08728
398.2'5 AACR2

Visit us on the World Wide Web!
www.harperchildrens.com

"The Thing" is adapted from an untitled story in *Bluenose Ghosts* by Helen Creighton with permission of McGraw-Hill Ryerson Ltd., Toronto. Copyright 1957 by The Ryerson Press.

"The Haunted House" is adapted from a story of that title in *American Folk Tales and Songs* by Richard Chase with permission of Dover Publications. Copyright 1956 by Richard Chase, 1971 by Dover Publications.

"Aaron Kelly's Bones" is adapted from "Daid Aaron II" in *Doctor to the Dead* by John Bennett with permission of Russell & Volkening, Inc., as agents for the author. Copyright 1943, 1971 by Mr. Bennett.

"Me Tie Dough-ty Walker!" is adapted from the tale "The Rash Dog and the Bloody Head," which appeared in the *Hoosier Folklore Bulletin*, vol. 1, 1942. Used by permission of Dr. Herbert Halpert, collector of the tale.

"Alligators" is adapted from "The Alligator Story" in *Sticks in the Knapsack and Other Ozark Folk Tales* by Vance Randolph with permission of the Columbia University Press. Copyright 1958 by the Columbia University Press.

"The White Wolf" is adapted from a story of that title in *The Telltale Lilac Bush and Other West Virginia Ghost Tales* by Ruth Ann Musick with permission of the University of Kentucky Press. Copyright 1965 by the University of Kentucky Press.

"A New Horse" is adapted from the tale "Bridling the Witch" in *Up Cutshin and Down Greasy: The Couches' Tales and Songs* (reprinted as *Sang Branch Settlers: Folksongs and Tales of an Eastern Kentucky Family*) by Leonard W. Roberts with permission of Dr. Roberts. Copyright 1980 by Leonard W. Roberts.

The musical notation on page 19 and page 40 was transcribed and illustrated by Melvin Wildberger.

Contents

4. *OTHER DANGERS*

5. *"AAAAAAAAAAAAH!"*

To Dinah

Scary Stories
to Tell in the Dark

Strange and Scary Things

Pioneers used to entertain themselves by telling scary stories. At night they might gather in somebody's cabin, or around a fire, and see who could scare the others the most.

Some girls and boys in my town do the same thing today. They get together at somebody's house, and they turn out the lights and eat popcorn, and scare one another half to death.

Telling scary stories is something people have done for thousands of years, for most of us *like* being scared in that way. Since there isn't any danger, we think it is fun.

There are a great many scary stories to tell. There are ghost stories. There are tales of witches, devils, bogeymen, zombies, and vampires. There are tales of monstrous creatures and of other dangers. There even are stories that make us laugh at all this scariness.

Some of these tales are very old, and they are told around the world. And most have the same origins. They are based on things that people saw or heard or experienced—or thought they did.

Many years ago a young prince became famous for a scary story he started to tell, but did not finish. His name was Mamillius, and he probably was nine or ten years old. William Shakespeare told about him in *The Winter's Tale.*

It was on a dark winter's day that his mother, the queen, asked him for a story.

"A sad tale's best for winter," he said. "I have one of sprites and goblins."

"Do your best to frighten me with your sprites," she said. "You're powerful at it."

"I shall tell it softly," he said. "Yond crickets shall not hear it."

And he began, "There was a man dwelt by a churchyard." But that was as far as he got. For at that moment the king came in and arrested the queen and took her away. And soon after that, Mamillius died. No one knows how he would have finished his story. If you started as he did, what would you tell?

Most scary stories are, of course, meant to be told. They are more scary that way. But *how* you tell them is important.

As Mamillius knew, the best way is to speak softly, so that your listeners lean forward to catch your words, and to speak slowly, so that your voice sounds scary.

And the best time to tell these stories is at night. In the dark and the gloom, it is easy for someone listening to imagine all sorts of strange and scary things.

Princeton, New Jersey — ALVIN SCHWARTZ

"Aaaaaaaaaaah!"

This chapter is filled with "jump stories" you can use to make your friends JUMP with fright.

· THE BIG TOE ·

A boy was digging at the edge of the garden when he saw a big toe. He tried to pick it up, but it was stuck to something. So he gave it a good hard jerk, and it came off in his hand. Then he heard something groan and scamper away.

The boy took the toe into the kitchen and showed it to his mother. "It looks nice and plump," she said. "I'll put it in the soup, and we'll have it for supper."

That night his father carved the toe into three pieces,

and they each had a piece. Then they did the dishes, and when it got dark they went to bed.

The boy fell asleep almost at once. But in the middle of the night, a sound awakened him. It was something out in the street. It was a voice, and it was calling to him.

"Where is my to-o-o-o-o-e?" it groaned.

When the boy heard that, he got very scared. But he thought, "It doesn't know where I am. It never will find me."

Then he heard the voice once more. Only now it was closer.

"Where is my to-o-o-o-o-e?" it groaned.

The boy pulled the blankets over his head and closed his eyes. "I'll go to sleep," he thought. "When I wake up it will be gone."

But soon he heard the back door open, and again he heard the voice.

"Where is my to-o-o-o-o-e?" it groaned.

Then the boy heard footsteps move through the kitchen into the dining room, into the living room, into the front hall. Then slowly they climbed the stairs.

Closer and closer they came. Soon they were in the upstairs hall. Now they were outside his door.

"Where is my to-o-o-o-o-e?" the voice groaned.

His door opened. Shaking with fear, he listened as the footsteps slowly moved through the dark toward his bed. Then they stopped.

"Where is my to-o-o-o-o-e?" the voice groaned.

(At this point, pause. Then jump at the person next to you and shout:)

"YOU'VE GOT IT!"

"The Big Toe" also has another ending.

When the boy hears the voice calling for its toe, he finds a strange-looking creature up inside the chimney. The boy is so frightened he can't move. He just stands there and stares at it.

Finally he asks: "W-w-w-what you got such big eyes for?"

And the creature answers: "To look you thro-o-o-ugh and thro-o-o-ugh!"

"W-w-w-what you got such big claws for?"

"To scra-a-a-tch up your gra-a-a-a-ve!"

"W-w-w-what you got such a big mouth for?"

"To swallow you who-o-o-le!"

"W-w-w-what you got such sharp teeth for?"

"TO CHOMP YOUR BONES!"

(As you give the last line, pounce on one of your friends.)

· *THE WALK* ·

My uncle was walking down a lonely dirt road one day. He came upon a man who also was walking down that road. The man looked at my uncle, and my uncle looked at the man. The man was scared of my uncle, and my uncle was scared of that man.

But they kept on walking, and it began to get dark. The man looked at my uncle, and my uncle looked at the man. The man was *very* scared of my uncle, and my uncle was *very* scared of that man.

But they kept on walking, and they came to a big woods. It was getting darker. And the man looked at my uncle, and my uncle looked at the man. The man was *really* scared of my uncle, and my uncle was *really* scared of that man.

But they kept on walking, and deep down into the woods they went. It was getting darker. And the man looked at my uncle, and my uncle looked at the man. The man was *terrible* scared of my uncle, and my uncle was *terrible* scared of—

(Now SCREAM!)

· *"WHAT DO YOU COME FOR?"* ·

There was an old woman who lived all by herself, and she was very lonely. Sitting in the kitchen one night, she said, "Oh, I wish I had some company."

No sooner had she spoken than down the chimney tumbled two feet from which the flesh had rotted. The old woman's eyes bulged with terror.

Then two legs dropped to the hearth and attached themselves to the feet.

Then a body tumbled down, then two arms, and a man's head.

As the old woman watched, the parts came together into a great, gangling man. The man danced around and around the room. Faster and faster he went. Then he stopped, and he looked into her eyes.

"What do you come for?" she asked in a small voice that shivered and shook.

"What do I come for?" he said. "I come—for YOU!"

(As you shout the last words, stamp your foot and jump at someone nearby.)

· *ME TIE DOUGH-TY WALKER!* ·

There was a haunted house where every night a bloody head fell down the chimney. At least that's what people said. So nobody would stay there overnight.

Then a rich man offered two hundred dollars to whoever would do it. And this boy said he would try if he could have his dog with him. So it was all settled.

The very next night the boy went to the house with his dog. To make it more cheerful, he started a fire in the fireplace. Then he sat in front of the fire and waited, and his dog waited with him.

For a while nothing happened. But a little after midnight he heard someone singing softly and sadly off in the woods. The singing sounded something like this:

"Me tie dough-ty walker!"

"It's just somebody singing," the boy told himself, but he was frightened.

Then his dog answered the song! Softly and sadly, it sang:

"Lynchee kinchy colly molly dingo dingo!"

The boy could not believe his ears. His dog had never uttered a word before. Then a few minutes later, he heard the singing again. Now it was closer and louder, but the words were the same:

"Me tie dough-ty walker!"

This time the boy tried to stop his dog from answering. He was afraid that whoever was singing would hear it and come after them.

But his dog paid no attention, and again it sang:

"Lynchee kinchy colly molly dingo dingo!"

A half-hour later the boy heard the singing again. Now it was in the back yard, and the song was the same:

"Me tie dough-ty walker!"

Again the boy tried to keep his dog quiet. But the dog sang out louder than ever:

"Lynchee kinchy colly molly dingo dingo!"

Soon the boy heard the singing again. Now it was coming down the chimney:

"Me tie dough-ty walker!"

The dog sang right back:

"Lynchee kinchy colly molly dingo dingo!"

Suddenly a bloody head fell out of the chimney. It missed the fire and landed right next to the dog. The dog took one look and fell over—dead from fright.

The head turned and stared at the boy. Slowly it opened its mouth, and—

(Turn to one of your friends and scream:)

"AAAAAAAAAAAH!"

A MAN WHO LIVED IN LEEDS

Some say this rhyme doesn't mean anything. Others are not so sure.

There was a man who lived in Leeds;
He filled his garden full of seeds.
And when the seeds began to grow,
It was like a garden filled with snow.
But when the snow began to melt,
It was like a ship without a belt.
And when the ship began to sail,
It was like a bird without a tail.
And when the bird began to fly,
It was like an eagle in the sky.
And when the sky began to roar,
It was like a lion at my door.
(Now drop your voice.)
And when the door began to crack,
It was like a penknife in my back.
And when my back began to bleed—
(Turn out any lights.)
I was dead, dead, dead *indeed!*
(Jump at your friends and scream:)
"AAAAAAAAAAAH!"

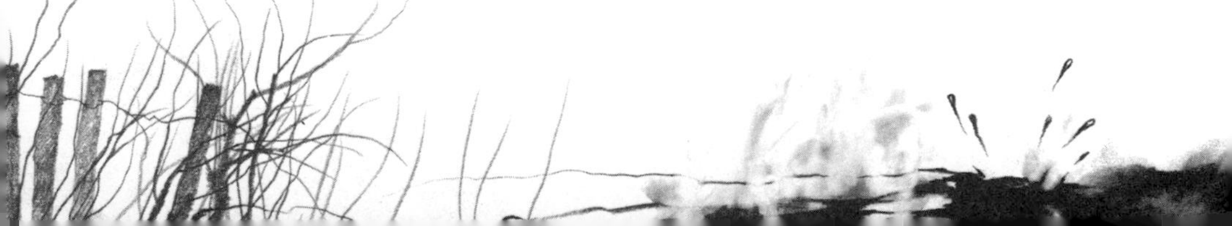

· OLD WOMAN ALL SKIN AND BONE ·

There was an old woman all skin and bone
Who lived near the graveyard all alone.
O-o o-o o-o!
She thought she'd go to church one day
To hear the parson preach and pray.
O-o o-o o-o!
And when she came to the church-house stile
She thought she'd stop and rest awhile.
O-o o-o o-o!
When she came up to the door
She thought she'd stop and rest some more.
O-o o-o o-o!
But when she turned and looked around
She saw a corpse upon the ground.
O-o o-o o-o!
From its nose down to its chin
The worms crawled out, and the worms crawled in.
O-o o-o o-o!
The woman to the preacher said,
"Shall I look like that when I am dead?"
O-o o-o o-o!
The preacher to the woman said,
"You'll look like that when you are dead!"
(Now scream:)
"AAAAAAAAAAAH!"

There was an old wo-man all skin and bone Who
lived near the grave-yard all a-lone. O-o o-o o-o!

He Heard Footsteps Coming Up the Cellar Stairs...

There are ghosts in this chapter. One comes back as a real person. Another takes revenge on her murderer. And there are other strange happenings.

THE THING ·

Ted Martin and Sam Miller were good friends. They spent a lot of time together. On this particular night they were sitting on a fence near the post office talking about one thing and another.

There was a field of turnips across the road. Suddenly they saw something crawl out of the field and stand up. It looked like a man, but in the dark it was hard to tell for sure. Then it was gone.

But soon it appeared again. It walked halfway across the road, then it turned around and went back into the field.

Then it came out a third time and started toward them. By now Ted and Sam were scared, and they started running. But when they finally stopped, they decided they were being foolish. They weren't sure what had scared them. So they decided to go back and get a better look.

Pretty soon they saw it, for it was coming to meet them. It was wearing black pants, a white shirt, and black suspenders.

Sam said, "I'm going to try to touch it. Then we'll know if it's real."

He walked up to it and peered into its face. It had bright penetrating eyes sunk deep in its head. It looked like a skeleton.

Ted took one look and screamed, and again he and Sam ran, but this time the skeleton followed them. When they got to Ted's house, they stood in the doorway and watched it. It stayed out in the road for a while. Then it disappeared.

A year later Ted got sick and died. Toward the end, Sam sat up with him every night. The night Ted died, Sam said he looked just like the skeleton.

· *COLD AS CLAY* ·

A farmer had a daughter for whom he cared more than anything on earth. She fell in love with a farmhand named Jim, but the farmer did not think Jim was good enough for his daughter. To keep them apart, he sent her to live with her uncle on the other side of the county.

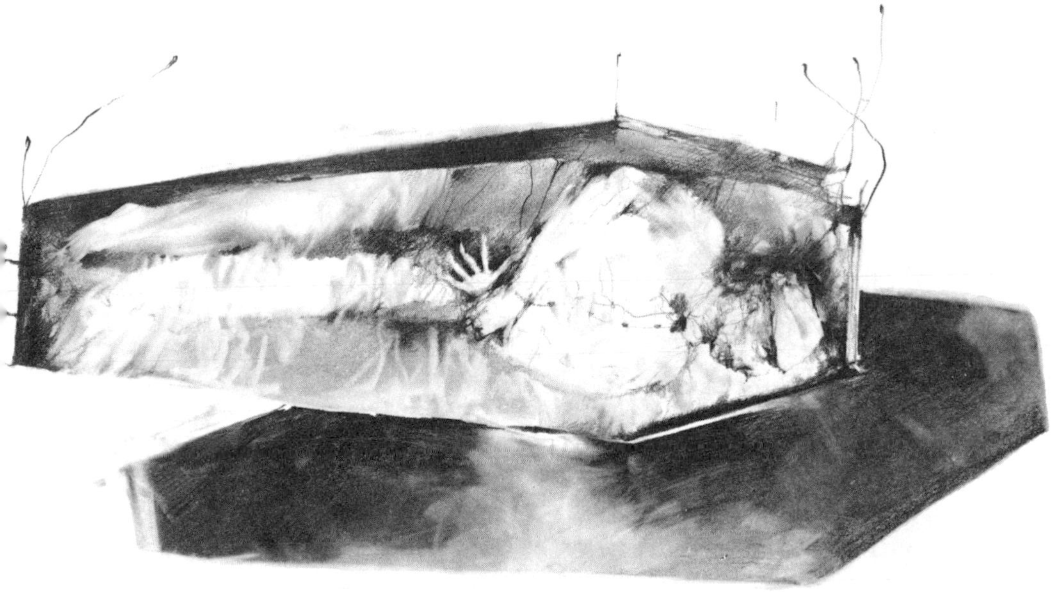

Soon after she left, Jim got sick, and he wasted away and died. Everyone said he died of a broken heart. The farmer felt so guilty about Jim's death, he could not tell his daughter what had happened. She continued to think about Jim and the life they might have had together.

One night many weeks later there was a knock on her uncle's door. When the girl opened the door, Jim was standing there.

"Your father asked me to get you," he said. "I came on his best horse."

"Is there anything wrong?" she asked.

"I don't know," he said.

She packed a few things, and they left. She rode behind him, clinging to his waist. Soon he complained of a headache. "It aches something terrible," he told her.

She put her hand on his forehead. "Why, you are as cold as clay," she said. "I hope you are not ill," and she wrapped her handkerchief around his head.

They traveled so swiftly that in a few hours they reached the farm. The girl quickly dismounted and knocked on the door. Her father was startled to see her.

"Didn't you send for me?" she asked.

"No, I didn't," he said.

She turned to Jim, but he was gone and so was the horse. They went to the stable to look for them. The horse was there. It was covered with sweat and trembling with fear. But there was no sign of Jim.

Terrified, her father told her the truth about Jim's death. Then quickly he went to see Jim's parents. They decided to open his grave. The corpse was in its coffin. But around its head they found the girl's handkerchief.

· *THE WHITE WOLF* ·

The timber wolves around French Creek had gotten out of hand. There were so many wolves, the farmers could not stop them from killing their cattle and sheep. So the state put a bounty on them. It would pay a hunter ten dollars for every wolf pelt he turned in.

A butcher in town named Bill Williams thought that was pretty good money. He stopped working as a butcher and started killing wolves. He was good at it. Every year he killed over five hundred of them. That came to more than five thousand dollars. It was quite a bit of money in those days.

After four or five years, Bill had killed so many wolves, there were hardly any left in that area. So he retired, and he vowed never to harm another wolf because wolves had made him rich.

Then one day a farmer reported that a white wolf had killed two of his sheep. He had shot at it and hit it, but the bullets didn't have any effect. Soon that wolf was seen all over the countryside, killing and running. But nobody could stop it.

One night it came into Bill's yard and killed his pet cow. Bill forgot about his decision never to harm another wolf. He went into town the next morning and bought a young lamb for bait. He took it out into the hills and tied it to a tree. Then he backed off about fifty yards and sat down under another tree. With his gun in his lap, he waited.

When Bill didn't come back, his friends started looking for him. Finally they found the lamb. It was still tied to a tree. It was hungry, but it was alive. Then they found Bill. He was still sitting against the other tree, but he was dead. His throat had been torn open.

But there was no sign of a struggle. His gun hadn't been fired. And there were no tracks in the soil around him. As for the white wolf, it was never seen again.

· *THE HAUNTED HOUSE* ·

One time a preacher went to see if he could put a haunt to rest at a house in his settlement. The house had been haunted for about ten years. Several people had tried to stay there all night, but they always would get scared out by the haunt.

So this preacher took his Bible and went to the house—went on in, built himself a good fire, and lit a lamp. Sat there reading the Bible. Then just before midnight he heard something start up in the cellar—walking back and forth, back and forth. Then it sounded like somebody was trying to scream and got choked off. Then there was a lot of thrashing around and struggling, and finally everything got quiet.

The old preacher took up his Bible again, but before he could start reading, he heard footsteps coming up the cellar stairs. He sat watching the door to the cellar, and the footsteps kept coming closer and closer. He saw the doorknob turn, and when the door began to open, he jumped up and hollered, "What do you want?"

The door shut back easy-like, and there wasn't a sound. The preacher was trembling a little, but he finally opened the Bible and read awhile. Then he got up and laid the book on the chair and went to mending the fire.

Then the haunt started walking again and—step!—step!—step!—up the cellar stairs. The old preacher sat watching the door, saw the doorknob turn and the door open. It looked like a young woman. He backed up and said, "Who are you? What do you want?"

The haunt sort of swayed like she didn't know what to do—then she just faded out. The old preacher waited, waited, and when he didn't hear any more noises, he went over and shut the door. He was sweating and trembling all over, but he was a brave man and he thought he'd be able to see it through. So he turned his chair to where he could watch, and he sat down and waited.

It wasn't long before he heard the haunt start up again, slowly—step!—step!—step!—step!—closer, and closer—step!—step!—and it was right at the door.

The preacher stood up and held his Bible out before him. Then the knob slowly turned, and the door opened wide. This time the preacher spoke quiet-like. He said, "In the name of the Father, the Son, and the Holy Ghost—who are you and what do you want?"

The haunt came right across the room, straight to him, and took hold of his coat. It was a young woman about twenty years old. Her hair was torn and tangled, and the flesh was dropping off her face so he could see the bones and part of her teeth. She had no eyeballs, but there was a sort of blue light way back in her eye sockets. And she had no nose to her face.

Then she started talking. It sounded like her voice was coming and going with the wind blowing it. She told how her lover had killed her for her money and buried her in the cellar. She said if the preacher would dig up her bones and bury her properly, she could rest.

Then she told him to take the end joint of the little finger from her left hand, and to lay it in the collection plate at the next church meeting—and he'd find out who had murdered her.

And she said, "If you come back here once more after that—you'll hear my voice at midnight, and I'll tell you where my money is hid, and you can give it to the church."

The haunt sobbed like she was tired, and she sunk down toward the floor and was gone. The preacher found her bones and buried them in the graveyard.

The next Sunday the preacher put the finger bone in the collection plate, and when a certain man happened to touch it, it stuck to his hand. The man jumped up and rubbed and scraped and tore at that bone, trying to get it off. Then he went to screaming, like he was going crazy. Well, he confessed to the murder, and they took him on to jail.

After the man was hung, the preacher went back to that house one midnight, and the haunt's voice told him to dig under the hearthrock. He did, and he found a big sack of money. And where that haunt had held on to his coat, the print of those bony fingers was burned right into the cloth. It never did come out.

· *THE GUESTS* ·

A young man and his wife were on a trip to visit his mother. Usually they arrived in time for supper. But they had gotten a late start, and now it was getting dark. So they decided to look for a place to stay overnight and go on in the morning.

Just off the road, they saw a small house in the woods. "Maybe they rent rooms," the wife said. So they stopped to ask.

An elderly man and woman came to the door. They didn't rent rooms, they said. But they would be glad to have them stay overnight as their guests. They had plenty of room, and they would enjoy the company.

The old woman made coffee and brought out some cake, and the four of them talked for a while. Then the young couple were taken to their room. They again explained that they wanted to pay for this, but the old man said he would not accept any money.

The young couple got up early the next morning before their hosts had awakened. On a table near the front door, they left an envelope with some money in it for the room. Then they went on to the next town.

They stopped in a restaurant and had breakfast. When they told the owner where they had stayed, he was shocked.

"That can't be," he said. "That house burned to the ground, and the man and the woman who lived there died in the fire."

The young couple could not believe it. So they went back to the house. Only now there was no house. All they found was a burned-out shell.

They stood staring at the ruins trying to understand what had happened. Then the woman screamed. In the rubble was a badly burned table, like the one they had seen by the front door. On the table was the envelope they had left that morning.

They Eat Your Eyes, They Eat Your Nose

There are scary stories about all kinds of things. The ones told here are about a grave, a witch, a man who liked to swim, a hunting trip, and a market basket. There also is one about worms eating a corpse—your corpse.

· *THE HEARSE SONG* ·

Don't you ever laugh as the hearse goes by,
For you may be the next to die.
They wrap you up in a big white sheet
From your head down to your feet.
They put you in a big black box
And cover you up with dirt and rocks.
All goes well for about a week,
Then your coffin begins to leak.
The worms crawl in, the worms crawl out,
The worms play pinochle on your snout.
They eat your eyes, they eat your nose,
They eat the jelly between your toes.
A big green worm with rolling eyes
Crawls in your stomach and out your eyes.
Your stomach turns a slimy green,
And pus pours out like whipping cream.
You spread it on a slice of bread,
And that's what you eat when you are dead.

Don't you ev - er laugh as the hearse goes by, For
you may be the next to die.

· THE GIRL WHO STOOD ON A GRAVE ·

Some boys and girls were at a party one night. There was a graveyard down the street, and they were talking about how scary it was.

"Don't ever stand on a grave after dark," one of the boys said. "The person inside will grab you. He'll pull you under."

"That's not true," one of the girls said. "It's just a superstition."

"I'll give you a dollar if you stand on a grave," said the boy.

"A grave doesn't scare me," said the girl. "I'll do it right now."

The boy handed her his knife. "Stick this knife in one of the graves," he said. "Then we'll know you were there."

The graveyard was filled with shadows and was as quiet as death. "There is nothing to be scared of," the girl told herself, but she was scared anyway.

She picked out a grave and stood on it. Then quickly she bent over and plunged the knife into the soil, and she started to leave. But she couldn't get away. Something was holding her back! She tried a second time to leave, but she couldn't move. She was filled with terror.

"Something has got me!" she screamed, and she fell to the ground.

When she didn't come back, the others went to look for her. They found her body sprawled across the grave. Without realizing it, she had plunged the knife through her skirt and had pinned it to the ground. It was only the knife that held her. She had died of fright.

· A NEW HORSE ·

Two farmhands shared a room. One slept at the back of the room. The other slept near the door. After a while, the one who slept near the door began to feel very tired early in the day. His friend asked what was wrong.

"An awful thing happens every night," he said. "A witch turns me into a horse and rides me all over the countryside."

"I'll sleep in your bed tonight," his friend said. "We'll see what happens to me."

About midnight an old woman who lived nearby came into the room. She mumbled some strange words over the farmhand, and he found he couldn't move. Then she slipped a bridle on him, and he turned into a horse.

The next thing he knew, she was riding him across the fields at breakneck speed, beating him to make him go even faster. Soon they came to a house where a party was going on. There was a lot of music and dancing. They were having a big time inside. She hitched him to a fence and went in.

While she was gone, the farmhand rubbed against the fence until the bridle came off, and he turned back into a human being.

Then he went into the house and found the witch. He spoke those strange words over her, and with the bridle he turned *her* into a horse. Then he rode her to a blacksmith and had her fitted with horseshoes. After that, he rode her to the farm where she lived.

"I have a pretty good filly here," he told her husband, "but I need a stronger horse. Would you like to trade?"

The old man looked her over, and he said he would do it. So they picked out another horse, and the farmhand rode away.

Her husband led his new horse to the barn. He took off the bridle and went to hang it up. But when he came back, the new horse was gone. Instead, there stood his wife with horseshoes nailed to her hands and feet.

· ALLIGATORS ·

A young woman in town married a man from another part of the country. He was a nice fellow, and they got along pretty well together. There was only one problem. Every night he'd go swimming in the river. Sometimes he would be gone all night long, and she would complain about how lonely she was.

This couple had two young sons. As soon as the boys could walk, their father began to teach them how to swim. And when they got to be old enough, he took them swimming in the river at night. Often they would stay there all night long, and the young woman would stay home all by herself.

After a while, she began to act in a strange way—at least, that is what the neighbors said. She told them that her husband was turning into an alligator, and that he was trying to turn the boys into alligators.

Everybody told her there was nothing wrong with a man taking his sons swimming. That was a natural thing to do. And when it came to alligators, there just weren't any nearby. Everybody knew that.

Early one morning the young woman came running into town from the direction of the river. She was soaking wet. She said a big alligator and two little alligators had pulled her in and had tried to get her to eat a raw fish. They were her husband and her sons, she said, and they wanted her to live with them. But she had gotten away.

Her doctor decided she had lost her mind, and he had

her put in the hospital for a while. After that nobody saw her husband and boys again. They just disappeared.

But now and then a fisherman would tell about seeing alligators in the river at night. Usually it was one big alligator and two small ones. But people said they were just making it up. Everybody knows there aren't any alligators around here.

· *ROOM FOR ONE MORE* ·

A man named Joseph Blackwell came to Philadelphia on a business trip. He stayed with friends in the big house they owned outside the city. That night they had a good time visiting. But when Blackwell went to bed, he tossed and turned and couldn't sleep.

Sometime during the night he heard a car turn into the driveway. He went to the window to see who was arriving at such a late hour. In the moonlight, he saw a long, black hearse filled with people.

The driver of the hearse looked up at him. When Blackwell saw his queer, hideous face, he shuddered. The driver called to him, "There is room for one more." Then he waited for a minute or two, and he drove off.

In the morning Blackwell told his friends what had happened. "You were dreaming," they said.

"I must have been," he said, "but it didn't seem like a dream."

After breakfast he went into Philadelphia. He spent the day high above the city in one of the new office buildings there.

Late in the afternoon he was waiting for an elevator to take him back down to the street. But when it arrived, it was very crowded. One of the passengers looked out and called to him. "There is room for one more," he said. It was the driver of the hearse.

"No, thanks," said Blackwell. "I'll get the next one."

The doors closed, and the elevator started down. There

was shrieking and screaming, then the sound of a crash. The elevator had fallen to the bottom of the shaft. Everyone aboard was killed.

· *THE WENDIGO* ·

A wealthy man wanted to go hunting in a part of northern Canada where few people had ever hunted. He traveled to a trading post and tried to find a guide to take him. But no one would do it. It was too dangerous, they said.

Finally, he found an Indian who needed money badly, and he agreed to take him. The Indian's name was DéFago.

They made camp in the snow near a large frozen lake. For three days they hunted, but they had nothing to show for it. The third night a windstorm came up. They lay in their tent listening to the wind howling and the trees whipping back and forth.

To see the storm better, the hunter opened the tent flap. What he saw startled him. There wasn't a breath of air stirring, and the trees were standing perfectly still. Yet he could *hear* the wind howling. And the more he listened, the more it sounded as if it were calling DéFago's name.

"Da-faaaaaaaaay-go!" it called. "Da-faaaaaaaaay-go!"

"I must be losing my mind," the hunter thought.

But DéFago had gotten out of his sleeping bag. He was huddled in a corner of the tent, his head buried in his arms.

"What's this all about?" the hunter asked.

"It's nothing," DéFago said.

But the wind continued to call to him. And DéFago became more tense and more restless.

"Da-Faaaaaaaaay-go!" it called. "Da-faaaaaaaaay-go!"

Suddenly, he jumped to his feet, and he began to run from the tent. But the hunter grabbed him and wrestled him to the ground.

"You can't leave me out here," the hunter shouted.

Then the wind called again, and DéFago broke loose and ran into the darkness. The hunter could hear him screaming as he went. Again and again he cried, "Oh, my fiery feet, my burning feet of fire . . ." Then his voice faded away, and the wind died down.

At daybreak, the hunter followed DéFago's tracks in the snow. They went through the woods, down toward the lake, then out onto the ice.

But soon he noticed something strange. The steps DéFago had taken got longer and longer. They were so long no human being could have taken them. It was as if something had helped him to hurry away.

The hunter followed the tracks out to the middle of the lake, but there they disappeared. At first, he thought that DéFago had fallen through the ice, but there wasn't any hole. Then he thought that something had pulled him off the ice into the sky. But that made no sense.

As he stood wondering what had happened, the wind

picked up again. Soon it was howling as it had the night before. Then he heard DéFago's voice. It was coming from up above, and again he heard DéFago screaming, ". . . My fiery feet, my burning feet . . ." But there was nothing to be seen.

Now the hunter wanted to leave that place as fast as he could. He went back to camp and packed. Then he left some food for DéFago, and he started out. Weeks later he reached civilization.

The following year he went back to hunt in that area again. He went to the same trading post to look for a guide. The people there could not explain what had happened to DéFago that night. But they had not seen him since then.

"Maybe it was the Wendigo," one of them said, and he laughed. "It's supposed to come with the wind. It drags you along at great speed until your feet are burned away, and more of you than that. Then it carries you into the sky, and it drops you. It's just a crazy story, but that's what some of the Indians say."

A few days later the hunter was at the trading post again. An Indian came in and sat by the fire. He had a blanket wrapped around him, and he wore his hat so that you couldn't see his face. The hunter thought there was something familiar about him.

He walked over and he asked, "Are you DéFago?"

The Indian didn't answer.

"Do you know anything about him?"

No answer.

He began to wonder if something was wrong, if the

man needed help. But he couldn't see his face.

"Are you all right?" he asked.

No answer.

To get a look at him, he lifted the Indian's hat. Then he screamed. There was nothing under the hat but a pile of ashes.

THE DEAD MAN'S BRAINS

This scary story is a scary game that people play at Hallowe'en. But it can be played whenever the spirit moves you.

The players sit in a circle in a darkened room and listen to a storyteller describe the rotting remains of a corpse. Each part is passed around for them to feel.

In one version, a player is out if he or she screams or gasps with fright. In another version, everybody stays to the end, no matter how scared they get.

Here is the story:

Once in this town there lived a man named Brown. It was years ago, on this night, that he was murdered out of spite.

We have here his remains.

First, let's feel his brains. (A wet, squishy tomato)

Now here are his eyes, still frozen with surprise. (Two peeled grapes)

This is his nose. (A chicken bone)

Here is his ear. (A dried apricot)

And here is his hand, rotting flesh and bone. (A cloth or rubber glove filled with mud or ice)

But his hair still grows. (A handful of corn silk or wet fur or yarn)

And his heart still beats, now and then. (A piece of raw liver)

And his blood still flows. Dip your fingers in it. It's nice and warm. (A bowl of catsup thinned with warm water)

That's all there is, except for these worms. They are the ones that ate the rest of him. (A handful of wet, cooked spaghetti noodles)

· "MAY I CARRY YOUR BASKET?" ·

Sam Lewis spent the evening playing chess at his friend's house. It was about midnight when they finished their game, and he started home. Outside it was icy cold and as quiet as the grave.

As he came around a turn in the road, he was surprised to see a woman walking ahead of him. She was carrying a basket covered with a white cloth. When he caught up to her, he looked to see who it was. But she was so bundled up against the cold, it was hard to see her face.

"Good evening," Sam said. "What brings you out so late?"

But she didn't answer.

Then he said, "May I carry your basket?"

She handed it to him. From under the cloth, a small voice said, "That's very nice of you," and that was followed by wild laughter.

Sam was so startled that he dropped the basket—and out rolled a woman's head. He looked at the head, and he stared at the woman. "It's *her* head!" he cried. And he started to run, and the woman and her head began to chase him.

Soon the head caught up to him. It bounded into the air and sunk its teeth into his left leg. Sam screamed with pain and ran faster.

But the woman and her head stayed right behind. Soon the head leaped into the air again and bit into his other leg. Then they were gone.

Other Dangers

Most of the scary stories in this book have been passed down over the years. But the ones in this chapter have been told only in recent times. They are stories that young people often tell about dangers we face in our lives today.

· THE HOOK ·

Donald and Sarah went to the movies. Then they went for a ride in Donald's car. They parked up on a hill at the edge of town. From there they could see the lights up and down the valley.

Donald turned on the radio and found some music. But an announcer broke in with a news bulletin. A murderer had escaped from the state prison. He was armed with a knife and was headed south on foot. His left hand was missing. In its place, he wore a hook.

"Let's roll up the windows and lock the doors," said Sarah.

"That's a good idea," said Donald.

"That prison isn't too far away," said Sarah. "Maybe we really should go home."

"But it's only ten o'clock," said Donald.

"I don't care what time it is," she said. "I want to go home."

"Look, Sarah," said Donald, "he's not going to climb all the way up here. Why would he do that? Even if he did, all the doors are locked. How could he get in?"

"Donald, he could take that hook and break through a window and open a door," she said. "I'm scared. I want to go home."

Donald was annoyed. "Girls always are afraid of something," he said.

As he started the car, Sarah thought she heard someone, or something, scratching at her door.

"Did you hear that?" she asked as they roared away. "It sounded like somebody was trying to get in."

"Oh, sure," said Donald.

Soon they got to her house.

"Would you like to come in and have some cocoa?" she asked.

"No," he said, "I've got to go home."

He went around to the other side of the car to let her out. Hanging on the door handle was a hook.

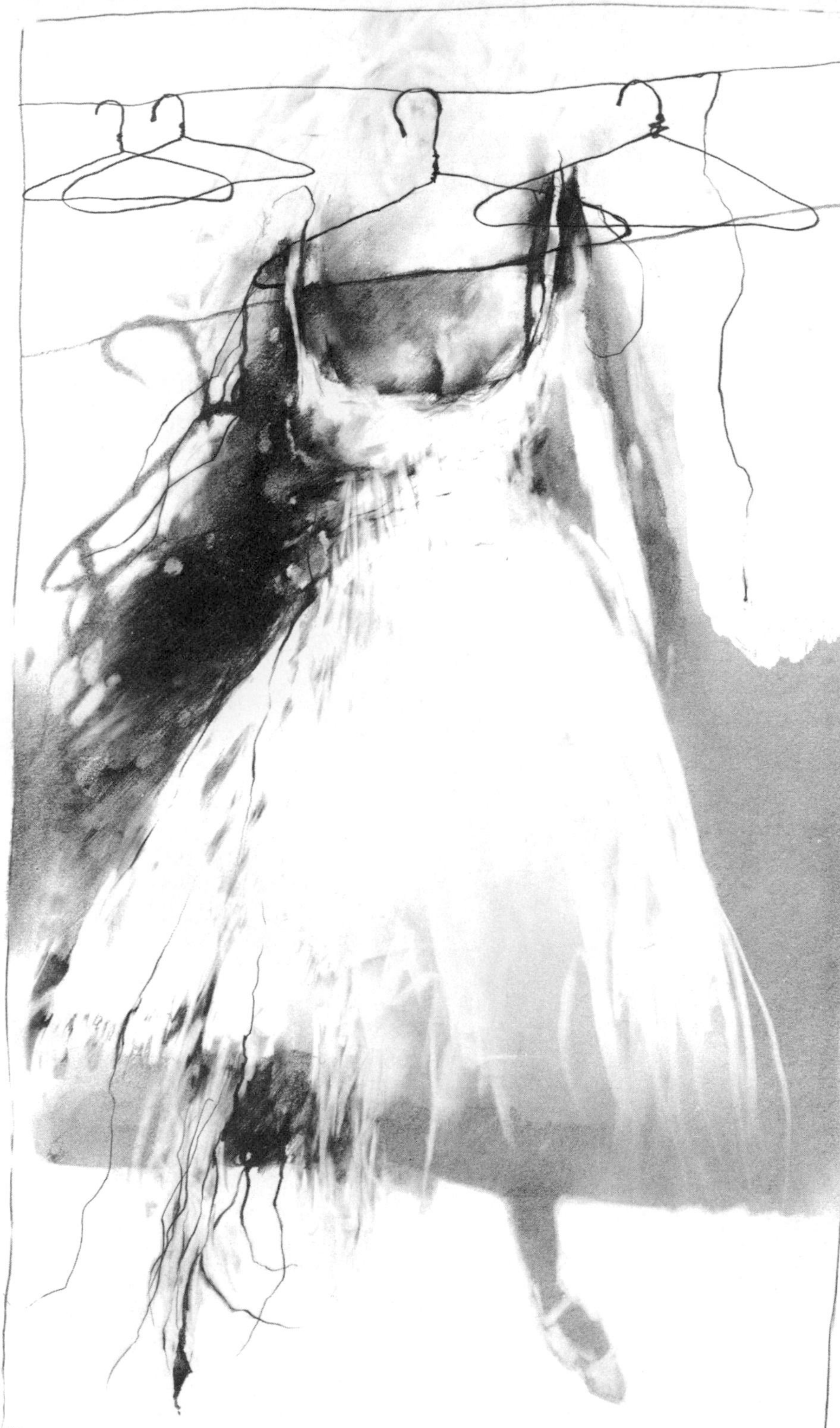

· THE WHITE SATIN EVENING GOWN ·

A young man invited a young woman to a formal dance. But she was very poor, and she could not afford to buy the evening gown she needed for such an occasion.

"Maybe you can rent a dress," her mother said. So she went to a pawnshop not far from where she lived. There she found a white satin evening gown in her size. She looked lovely in it, and she was able to rent it for very little.

When she arrived at the dance with her friend, she was so attractive, everyone wanted to meet her. She danced again and again and was having a wonderful time. But then she began to feel dizzy and faint, and she asked her friend to take her home. "I think I have danced too much," she told him.

When she got home, she lay down on her bed. The next morning her mother found that her daughter had died. The doctor did not understand what had caused her death. So he had the coroner perform an autopsy.

The coroner found that she had been poisoned by embalming fluid. It had stopped her blood from flowing. There were traces of the fluid on her dress. He decided it had entered her skin when she perspired while she was dancing.

The pawnbroker said he bought the dress from an undertaker's helper. It had been used in a funeral for another young woman, and the helper had stolen it just before she was buried.

· *HIGH BEAMS* ·

The girl driving the old blue sedan was a senior at the high school. She lived on a farm about eight miles away and used the car to drive back and forth.

She had driven into town that night to see a basketball game. Now she was on her way home. As she pulled away from the school, she noticed a red pick-up truck follow her out of the parking lot. A few minutes later the truck was still behind her.

"I guess we're going in the same direction," she thought.

She began to watch the truck in her mirror. When she changed her speed, the driver of the truck changed his speed. When she passed a car, so did he.

Then he turned on his high beams, flooding her car with light. He left them on for almost a minute. "He probably wants to pass me," she thought. But she was becoming uneasy.

Usually she drove home over a back road. Not too many people went that way. But when she turned onto that road, so did the truck.

"I've got to get away from him," she thought, and she began to drive faster. Then he turned his high beams on again. After a minute, he turned them off. Then he turned them on again and off again.

She drove even faster, but the truck driver stayed right behind her. Then he turned his high beams on again. Once more her car was ablaze with light. "What *is* he doing?" she wondered. "What *does* he want?" Then he turned them off again. But a minute later he had them on again, and he left them on.

At last she pulled into her driveway, and the truck pulled in right behind her. She jumped from the car and ran to the house. "Call the police!" she screamed at her father. Out in the driveway she could see the driver of the truck. He had a gun in his hand.

When the police arrived, they started to arrest him, but he pointed to the girl's car. "You don't want me," he said. "You want him."

Crouched behind the driver's seat, there was a man with a knife.

As the driver of the truck explained it, the man slipped into the girl's car just before she left the school. He saw it happen, but there was no way he could stop it. He thought about getting the police, but he was afraid to leave her. So he followed her car.

Each time the man in the back seat reached up to overpower her, the driver of the truck turned on his high beams. Then the man dropped down, afraid that someone might see him.

· *THE BABYSITTER* ·

It was nine o'clock in the evening. Everybody was sitting on the couch in front of the TV. There were Richard, Brian, Jenny, and Doreen, the babysitter.

The telephone rang.

"Maybe it's your mother," said Doreen. She picked up the phone. Before she could say a word, a man laughed hysterically and hung up.

"Who was it?" asked Richard.

"Some nut," said Doreen. "What did I miss?"

At nine-thirty the telephone rang again. Doreen answered it. It was the man who had called before. "I'll be there soon," he said, and he laughed and hung up.

"Who was it?" the children asked.

"Some crazy person," she said.

About ten o'clock the telephone rang again. Jenny got to it first.

"Hello," she said.

It was the same man. "One more hour," he said, and he laughed and hung up.

"He said, 'One more hour.' What did he mean?" asked Jenny.

"Don't worry," said Doreen. "It's somebody fooling around."

"I'm scared," said Jenny.

About ten-thirty the telephone rang once more. When Doreen picked it up, the man said, "Pretty soon now," and he laughed.

"*Why* are you doing this?" Doreen screamed, and he hung up.

"Was it that guy again?" asked Brian.

"Yes," said Doreen. "I'm going to call the operator and complain."

The operator told her to call back if it happened again,

and she would try to trace the call.

At eleven o'clock the telephone rang again. Doreen answered it. "Very soon now," the man said, and he laughed and hung up.

Doreen called the operator. Almost at once she called back. "That person is calling from a telephone upstairs," she said. "You'd better leave. I'll get the police."

Just then a door upstairs opened. A man they had never seen before started down the stairs toward them. As they ran from the house, he was smiling in a very strange way. A few minutes later, the police found him there and arrested him.

"Aaaaaaaaaaah!"

This chapter has the same title as the first chapter. But the stories in the first chapter are meant to scare you. The ones in this chapter are meant to make you laugh.

· THE VIPER ·

A widow lived alone on the top floor of an apartment house. One morning her telephone rang.

"Hello," she said.

"This is the viper," a man said. "I'm coming up."

"Somebody is fooling around," she thought, and hung up.

A half-hour later the telephone rang again. It was the same man.

"It's the viper," he said. "I'll be up soon."

The widow didn't know what to think, but she was getting frightened.

Once more the telephone rang. Again it was the viper.

"I'm coming up now," he said.

She quickly called the police. They said they would be right over. When the doorbell rang, she sighed with relief. "They are here!" she thought.

But when she opened the door, there stood a little old man with a bucket and a cloth. "I am the viper," he said. "I vish to vash and vipe the vindows."

· *THE ATTIC* ·

A man named Rupert lived with his dog in a house deep in the woods. Rupert was a hunter and a trapper. The dog was a big German shepherd named Sam. Rupert had raised Sam from a pup.

Almost every morning Rupert went hunting, and Sam stayed behind and guarded the house. One morning, as Rupert was checking his traps, he got the feeling that something was wrong at home.

He hurried back as fast as he could, but when he got there he found that Sam was missing. He searched the house and the woods nearby, but Sam was nowhere to be seen. He called and he called, but the dog did not answer. For days Rupert looked for Sam, but he could find no trace of him.

Finally he gave up and went back to his work. But one morning he heard something moving in the attic. He picked up his gun. Then he thought, "I'd better be quiet about this."

So he took off his boots. And in his bare feet he began to climb the attic stairs. He slowly took one step—then another—then another, until at last he reached the attic door.

He stood outside listening, but he didn't hear a thing. Then he opened the door, and—

"AAAAAAAAAAH!"

(At this point, the storyteller stops, as if he has finished. Then usually somebody will ask, "Why did Rupert scream?"

The storyteller replies, "You'd scream too if you stepped on a nail in your bare feet.")

· THE SLITHERY-DEE ·

The slithery-dee,
He came out of the sea;

He ate all the others,
But he didn't eat me.

The slithery-dee,
He came out of the sea;

He ate all the others,
But he didn't eat—
SL-U-R-P . . .

HOW THAT DEAD MAN DANCED!

· *AARON KELLY'S BONES* ·

Aaron Kelly was dead. They bought him a coffin and had a funeral and buried him.

But that night he got out of his coffin, and he came home. His family was sitting around the fire when he walked in.

He sat down next to his widow, and he said, "What's going on? You all act like somebody died. Who's dead?"

His widow said, "You are."

"I don't feel dead," he said. "I feel fine."

"You don't look fine," his widow said. "You look dead. You'd better get back to the grave where you belong."

"I'm not going back to the grave until I *feel* dead," he said.

Since Aaron wouldn't go back, his widow couldn't collect his life insurance. Without that, she couldn't pay for the coffin. And the undertaker said he would take it back.

Aaron didn't care. He just sat by the fire rocking in

a chair and warming his hands and feet. But his joints were dry and his back was stiff, and every time he moved, he creaked and cracked.

One night the best fiddler in town came to court the widow. Since Aaron was dead, the fiddler wanted to marry her. The two of them sat on one side of the fire, and Aaron sat on the other side, creaking and cracking.

"How long do we have to put up with this dead corpse?" the widow asked.

"Something must be done," the fiddler said.

"This isn't very jolly," Aaron said. "Let's dance!"

The fiddler got out his fiddle and began to play. Aaron stretched himself, shook himself, got up, took a step or two, and began to dance.

With his old bones rattling, and his yellow teeth snapping, and his bald head wagging, and his arms flip-flopping—around and around he went.

With his long legs clicking, and his kneebones knocking, he skipped and pranced around the room. How that dead man danced! But pretty soon a bone worked loose and fell to the floor.

"Look at that!" said the fiddler.

"Play faster!" said the widow.

The fiddler played faster.

Crickety-crack, down and back, the dead man went hopping, and his dry bones kept dropping—this way, that way, the pieces just kept popping.

"Play, man! Play!" cried the widow.

The fiddler fiddled, and dead Aaron danced. Then Aaron fell apart, collapsed into a pile of bones—all except his bald headbone *that* grinned at the fiddler, cracked its teeth—and kept dancing.

"Look at that!" groaned the fiddler.

"Play louder!" cried the widow.

"Ho, ho!" said the headbone. "Ain't we having fun!"

The fiddler couldn't stand it. "Widow," he said. "I'm going home," and he never came back.

The family gathered up Aaron's bones and put them back in the coffin. They mixed them up so he couldn't fit them together. After that, Aaron stayed in his grave.

But his widow never did get married again. Aaron had seen to that.

· WAIT TILL MARTIN COMES ·

An old man was out for a walk. When a storm came up, he looked for a place to take shelter. Soon he came to an old house. He ran up on the porch and knocked on the door, but nobody answered.

By now rain was pouring down, thunder was booming, and lightning was flashing. So he tried the door. When he found it was unlocked, he went inside.

Except for a pile of wooden boxes, the house was empty. He broke up some of the boxes and made a fire with them. Then he sat down in front of the fire and dried himself. It was so warm and cozy that he fell asleep.

When he woke up a black cat was sitting near the fire. It stared at him for a while. Then it purred. "That's a nice cat," he thought, and he dozed off again.

When he opened his eyes, there was a second cat in the room. But this one was as big as a wolf. It looked at him very closely, and it asked, "Shall we do it now?"

"No," said the other cat. "Let's wait till Martin comes."

"I must be dreaming," thought the old man. He closed his eyes again. Then he took another look. But now there was a *third* cat in the room, and this one was as big as a tiger. It looked the old man over, and it asked, "Shall we do it now?"

"No," said the others. "Let's wait till Martin comes."

The old man jumped up, jumped out the window and started running. "When Martin comes, you tell him I couldn't wait," he called.

· THE GHOST WITH THE BLOODY FINGERS ·

A businessman arrived at a hotel late one night and asked for a room. The room clerk told him the hotel was all filled up. "There is only one empty room," he said. "But we don't rent that one because it is haunted."

"I'll take it," said the businessman. "I don't believe in ghosts."

The man went up to the room. He unpacked his things, and he went to bed. As soon as he did, a ghost came out of the closet. Its fingers were bleeding, and it was moaning, "Bloody fingers! Bloody fingers!" When the man saw the ghost, he grabbed his things and ran.

The next night a woman arrived very late. Again, all the rooms were taken except the haunted room.

"I'll sleep there," she said. "I'm not afraid of ghosts."

As soon as she got into bed, the ghost came out of the closet. Its fingers still were bleeding. It still was moaning, "Bloody fingers! Bloody fingers!" And the woman took one look and ran.

A week later another guest arrived very late. He also took the haunted room.

After he unpacked, he got out his guitar and he began to play. Soon the ghost appeared. As before, its fingers were bleeding, and it was moaning, "Bloody fingers! Bloody fingers!"

The man paid no attention. He just kept strumming his guitar. But the ghost kept moaning, and its fingers kept bleeding.

Finally, the guitar player looked up. "Cool it, man!" he said. "Get yourself a Band-Aid."

ABBREVIATIONS IN NOTES, SOURCES, AND BIBLIOGRAPHY

CFQ	*California Folklore Quarterly*
HF	*Hoosier Folklore*
HFB	*Hoosier Folklore Bulletin*
IF	*Indiana Folklore*
JAF	*Journal of American Folklore*
KFQ	*Kentucky Folklore Quarterly*
MFA	Maryland Folklore Archive, University of Maryland, College Park, Md.
NEF	*Northeast Folklore*
NMFR	*New Mexico Folklore Record*
NYFQ	*New York Folklore Quarterly*
PTFS	Publication of the Texas Folklore Society
RU	Compiler's collection of folklore, contributed by his students at Rutgers University, New Brunswick, N.J., 1963–78.
SFQ	*Southern Folklore Quarterly*
UMFA	University of Massachusetts Folklore Archive, Amherst, Mass.
WSFA	Wayne State University Folklore Archive, Detroit, Mich.

Notes

The publications cited are described in the Bibliography.

Jump stories (pp. 5–18): There are dozens of jump stories, but today only two are widely known. One is "The Big Toe," which appears in Chapter 1 and circulates in southeastern United States. The other is "The Golden Arm," from which "The Big Toe" derives.

In "The Golden Arm," a man marries a woman who wears a beautifully crafted golden arm. When she dies, he steals it from her grave, only to have her ghost return to claim it. In some variants, it is a golden heart he steals or golden hair or diamond eyes. Or it is a natural organ, usually the liver or the heart, that he eats, despite the cannibalism involved.

"The Big Toe" is an American tale. "The Golden Arm," although widely used in the United States, has English and German antecedents. The Grimm brothers reported a version of it early in the nineteenth century, but the tale predates that period.

Mark Twain used to tell "The Golden Arm" in his public performances. Here is some advice he once gave on delivering the jump lines that he once gave. It also applies to the telling of "The Big Toe."

"You must wail ['Who's got my golden arm?'] very plaintively and accusingly; then you [pause, and you] stare steadily and impressively into the face of . . . a girl, preferably—and let that awe-inspiring pause build into a deep hush. When it has reached exactly the right length, jump suddenly at that girl and yell, *'You've* got it!'

"If you got your pause right, she'll fetch a dear little yelp and spring right out of her shoes. . . ."

There are three approaches to telling these jump stories. Two are found in Chapter 1. In the third approach, the ghost returns to search for what has been stolen. Feigning innocence, the grave robber asks what has become of various parts of the ghost's body. To each question, the ghost replies, "All withered and wasted away." When the robber mentions the part of the body that was stolen, the ghost shrieks, *"You've* got it!" See Botkin, *American,* pp. 502–503; Burrison; Roberts, *Old Greasybeard,* pp. 33–36; Stimson, *JAF* 58:126.

Ghosts (pp. 21–34): In almost every civilization, there has been a belief that the dead return. They are said to come back for various reasons. Their lives were ended before their "allotted time." They did not receive a proper burial. They had important business to finish or a responsibility to meet. They wished to punish somebody or to take revenge. Or they wanted to comfort or advise someone, or obtain forgiveness.

It is said that some return as human beings. In fact, they may look just as they did when they were alive, and people they meet may not realize they are ghosts.

One of the best known of these "living ghosts" is the ghostly or vanishing hitchhiker. It usually is late at night that a motorist encounters her. She is standing on a street corner or at the side of a road, and she asks to be taken home.

She sits in the back seat of the car. But when the driver finds the address he has been given, he discovers that she has vanished. When he informs her family of this, he learns that she died on that night several years before at the spot where he picked her up.

There are two stories about living ghosts in Chapter 2: "The Guests" and "Cold as Clay."

Some persons who die are said to return as animals, particularly as dogs. Other ghosts may have a spectral quality. Or they may appear as a ball of fire or as a moving light. Or they may make their presence known through sounds they make or actions they take, such as slamming a door, rattling a key in a lock, or moving furniture.

The ghosts of animals also have been reported, as have the ghosts of objects such as guns, boots, and rifles, and trains and cars associated with death.

Ghosts of human beings do many things a human does. They eat, drink, ride on trains and buses, play the piano, and go fishing. They also laugh, cry, shout, whisper, and make all sorts of noises.

When it has completed what it set out to do, a ghost is likely to return to its grave. But at times this may require the help of a person, such as a minister, who may be experienced in "laying" ghosts, or putting them to rest.

If you wish to see or hear a ghost, these are some recommended approaches: Look back over your left shoulder. Look through either one of a mule's ears. Look in a mirror with another person. Arrange six pure white dinner plates around a table, then go to a cemetery at noon and call the name of someone you once knew who is buried there.

If you encounter a ghost, it is advised that you speak to it. If you do so, you may be able to help it finish whatever it is doing and return to its grave. Some say it is most effective if you address a ghost this way: "In the name of God [or in the name of the Father, the Son, and the Holy Ghost], what do you want?" They also say that holding a Bible will protect you against a revengeful ghost and demonstrate your sincerity.

However, most ghosts are not regarded as dangerous. As the folklorist Maria Leach pointed out, "Usually a ghost is some poor harmless soul . . . looking for someone with enough understanding and kindness to speak to it and do it some little favor." See Beardsley and Hankie, *CFQ* 1:303–36; *CFQ* 2:3–25; Creighton, pp. i–xi; Hole, pp. 1–12; Gardner, p. 85; Leach, *Dictionary,* "Revenant," pp. 933–34; Leach, *Thing,* pp. 9–11.

"The Thing" (pp. 23–24): This tale describes a forerunner, or a forewarning of death. The warning is a skeletonlike figure that appears, then chases the principal characters. The skeleton actually is a "wraith," an apparition that depicts a living person as he or she will look at death. But the most commonly reported forerunners are heard, not seen. They are sounds like a knock on the door or the striking of a clock. See Creighton, pp. 1–7, 69–70.

"The Haunted House" (pp. 29–32): The tale of a person who is brave enough to spend a night in a haunted house, and who often is rewarded for his bravery, is told again and again around the world. There are many versions of this story, but the theme never changes. In this book there are four disparate variants of this tale: "Me Tie Dough-ty Walker!" "The Haunted House," "Wait till Martin Comes," and "The Ghost with the Bloody Fingers." The tale is classified as Type 326 (the youth who wanted to know what fear was). See Ives, *NEF* 4:61–67; Roberts, *Old Greasybeard,* pp. 72–74, 187; Roberts, *South,* pp. 35–38, 217–18.

"The Hearse Song" (p. 39): Although many adults are familiar with this song, it is best known in the elementary schools. But during World War I, it was a war song that was sung by servicemen from America and England. One version went this way:

"Did you ever think as the hearse rolls by
That some of these days you must surely die?
They'll take you away in a big black hack;
They'll take you away but they won't bring you back.

". . . And your eyes drop out and your teeth fall in
And the worms crawl over your mouth and chin;
And the worms crawl out and the worms crawl in
And your limbs drop off limb by limb."

The words have changed quite a bit since then. Worms now play pinochle on your snout. There is jelly between your toes. And pus, like whipping cream, pours out of your stomach.

With children as the audience, it is a more gruesome song, but it is not as grim. One scholar associates the change of words with a change of function. During World War I, the song helped servicemen deal with the fear they felt. These days it helps children confirm the reality of death, yet through satire and humor deny its reality for them.

The song is part of an old poetic tradition. During the Middle Ages many of the poems written in European countries dealt with death and decay. Here is a verse of this type from a twelfth-century poem, which has been translated from the Middle English:

"A vicious worm lives in my backbone;
My eyes are dazed and very dim;
My guts rot, my hair is green,
My teeth grin very grimly."

At that time such poems may have served still another purpose: turning one's thoughts from the flesh to the hereafter. See Doyle, PTFS 40:175–90; for two World War I versions of "The Hearse Song," see Sandburg, p. 444.

"The Wendigo" (pp. 49–53): The Wendigo, or Windigo, is a female spirit that personifies the awful cold of the northern forests. She figures in the folklore of forest Indians in Canada

and in sections of northernmost United States.

According to this legend, the Wendigo attracts victims by calling to them in an irresistible way, then bears them away at great speed, finally sweeps them into the sky, then drops them, leaving them with frozen stumps where their feet once were. As they are carried off, they characteristically scream, ". . . My fiery feet, my burning feet of fire!"

The only defense against the Wendigo is to restrain the person who is being called. But the spirit then tries to entice whoever is holding him. See Crowe, *NMFR* 11:22–23.

In the lore of some northern tribes, the Wendigo functions not as the spirit of the cold, but as a cannibal giant that kills for human flesh. Some nineteenth-century Indians also suffered a compulsion to eat human flesh, an illness anthropologists later described as a "Windigo psychosis." See Speck, *JAF* 48:81–82; Brown, *American Anthropologist* 73:20–21.

Belief legends (pp. 59–71): The stories in Chapter 4 are not hard to believe. They deal with ordinary people. They describe incidents that do not seem beyond the realm of possibility.

But the same incidents are reported again and again at locations in different parts of the country. And it is never possible to trace these stories to the actual participants. The closest one usually comes is a report from someone who knew someone who knew those involved.

(The one known exception involves the legend of a "death car," a late model automobile that was sold for virtually nothing because of the smell of a corpse that cannot be removed. The folklorist Richard M. Dorson traced the origins of the story to Mecosta, Michigan, where the incident occurred in 1938).

Most of these stories are expressions of the anxiety people have about certain aspects of their lives. They evolve from incidents and rumors that reinforce these fears, and around which stories are constructed.

These modern legends are described by folklorists as "migratory belief legends." They are "migratory" in the sense that they do not attach themselves to single locations, as traditional legends often do. They are among the most vigorous of modern folklorist forms.

All the stories in Chapter 4 are belief legends about some of the dangers that might confront a young person. The story "Room for One More," in Chapter 3, is another belief legend. It is concerned with the supernatural, but it has been reported in several locations in the United States and the British Isles.

These legends also are concerned with violence, horror, threats posed by technology, impurity of food, relationships with friends and relatives, personal embarrassment, and other sources of anxiety.

They circulate by word of mouth, but at times the media carry reports that further disseminates them. See Brunvand, *American,* pp. 110–12; Brunvand, *Urban American Legends;* Dégh, " 'Belief Legend,' " pp. 56–68.

"The White Satin Evening Gown" (p. 65): Two versions of this story were known in ancient Greece. Hercules dies when he wears a robe his wife poisoned with the blood of his rival, the centaur Nessus. Medea sends a gift of a poisoned robe to Creusa, the woman her former husband, Jason, intends to marry. When Creusa tries on the robe, she dies. See Himelick, *HF* 5:83–84.

Sources

The source of each item is given, along with variants and related information. Where available, the names of collectors (C) and informants (I) are given. Publications cited are described in the Bibliography.

STRANGE AND SCARY THINGS

p. 3 *"There was a man dwelt . . .":* Prince Mamillius begins to tell his tale in Act II, Scene 1, of *The Winter's Tale.* The lines quoted have been rearranged slightly for clarity. See Shakespeare, p. 1107.

1. "AAAAAAAAAAAH!"

p. 7 *"The Big Toe:"* These are variants of "The Big Toe," a traditional story which is widespread in southern United States. I learned them while serving in the U.S. Navy during World War II. My informant was a sailor from either Virginia or West Virginia. The tales are retold from memory. For parallels, see Boggs, *JAF* 47:296; Chase, *American,* pp. 57–59; Chase, *Grandfather,* pp. 22–26; Kennedy, PTFS 6:41–42; Roberts, *South,* pp. 52–54.

p. 11 *"The Walk":* (I) Edward Knowlton, Stonington, Maine, 1976. For a parallel, see "Ma Uncle Sandy," a Scottish tale that ends with the jump word "WOW!" in Briggs, *Dictionary,* Part A, vol. 2, p. 542.

p. 12 *"What Do You Come For?":* This is a retelling of a tale told in America and in the British Isles. See Bacon, *JAF* 35:290; Boggs, *JAF* 47:296–97. For a nineteenth-century Scottish version, "The Strange Visitor," see Chambers, pp. 64–65.

p. 14 *"Me Tie Dough-ty Walker!":* This is a retelling of a Kentucky tale collected by Herbert Halpert in Bloomington, Indiana, in 1940. The informant was Mrs. Otis Milby Melcher. For Dr. Halpert's transcription of the tale and an interview with the informant, see *HFB* 1:9–11. The story appears under the title "The Rash Dog and the Bloody Head." It has been expanded slightly, in line with the informant's published suggestions for telling. The ending also has been modified slightly. In the original ending, the storyteller pauses after the dog dies, then shouts "BOO!" Several children who heard the story didn't think the ending was scary enough. Bill Tucker, twelve, and Billy Green, twelve, of Bangor, Maine, suggested the change. Motif: H. 1411.1 (fear test: staying in a haunted house where a corpse drops piecemeal down the chimney). For related haunted house tales, see Boggs, *JAF* 47:296–97; Ives, *NEF* 4:61–67; Randolph, *Turtle,* pp. 22–23; Roberts, *South,* pp. 35–38. In this book, see "The Haunted House," pp. 29–32.

p. 17 *"A Man Who Lived in Leeds":* (I) Tom O'Brien, San Francisco, 1975. The informant learned this from his English father around the turn of the century. For an English parallel, see Blakesborough, p. 258.

p. 18 *"Old Woman All Skin and Bone":* A traditional song and tale in America and the British Isles. For variants, see Belden, pp. 502–503; Chase, *American,* p. 186; Cox, *Folk-Songs,* pp. 482–83; Flanders, 180–81; Stimson, *JAF* 58:126.

2. HE HEARD FOOTSTEPS COMING UP THE CELLAR STAIRS . . .

p. 23 *"The Thing":* This tale of a forerunner of death is based on an account in Helen Creighton's book, *Bluenose Ghosts,* pp. 4–6.

p. 25 *"Cold as Clay":* This is a tale told both in America and England. It is based on the English ballad "The Suffolk Miracle." See Child, vol. 5, no. 272, p. 66. For a text of the tale as it was told in Virginia, see Gainer, pp. 62–63. Motif: E.210 (dead lover's malevolent return).

p. 27 *"The White Wolf":* This is a retelling of an incident reported by Ruth Ann Musick in *The Telltale Lilac Bush and Other West Virginia Ghost Stories,* pp. 134–35. (I) Lester Tinnell, French Creek, West Virginia, 1954. Motifs: E.423.2.7 (revenant as wolf); E.320 (return from dead to inflict punishment).

p. 29 *"The Haunted House":* This story was reported by Richard Chase in *American Folk Tales and Songs,* pp. 60–63. He collected it in Wise County, Virginia, prior to 1956. Abridged slightly for clarity.

p. 33 *"The Guests":* This story has been told in many places. At one time it was well known in the area around Albany, New York. The version in this book is based on two sources: the recollection of my wife, Barbara Carmer Schwartz, who grew up in the Albany area, and an account reported by Louis C. Jones in *Things That Go Bump in the Night,* pp. 76–78. Dr. Jones's informant was Sunna Cooper.

3. THEY EAT YOUR EYES, THEY EAT YOUR NOSE

p. 39 *"The Hearse Song":* Variant of a traditional song, Brooklyn, New York, 1940s. For a compilation of variants, see Doyle, PTFS 40:175–90.

p. 41 *"The Girl Who Stood on a Grave":* This is a retelling of an old tale that is well known in America and the British Isles. In other versions, the victim is pinned by a stick, a post, a croquet stake, a sword, and a fork. See Boggs, *JAF* 47:295–96; Roberts, *South,* 136–37; Montell, 200–201. Motifs: H.1416.1 (fear test: visiting a graveyard at night); N.334 (accidental fatal ending of game or joke).

p. 43 *"A New Horse":* This witch tale has been told all over the world. The retelling in this book is based on a tale from the Kentucky mountains reported by Leonard Roberts. In that version the old man takes a gun and blows his wife's brains out after he realizes she is a witch. See Roberts, *Up Cutshin,* pp. 128–29.

p. 45 *"Alligators":* This story is based on an Ozark tale Vance Randolph reported as "The Alligator Story" in *Sticks in the Knapsack,* pp. 22–23. He collected it from an elderly woman at Willow Springs, Missouri, in August 1939.

p. 47 *"Room for One More":* RU, 1970. This legend has circulated for many years in the United States and the British Isles. For two English versions, see Briggs, *Dictionary,* vol. 2, pp. 545–46, 575–76.

p. 49 *"The Wendigo":* This Indian tale also is a summer camp tale that is well known in northeastern United States. It is adapted from a version that Professor Edward M. Ives of the University of Maine narrated for me. He first heard it in the 1930s when he attended Camp Curtis Read, a Boy Scout camp near Mahopac, New York. For a literary version of this tale, see "The Wendigo" by the English author Algernon Blackwood, in Davenport, pp. 1–58. The name DéFago used in the above adaptation is taken from this story.

p. 54 *"The Dead Man's Brains":* The first paragraph of the story, MFA, 1975. The rest is so widely known, it is not based on any particular version.

p. 56 *"May I Carry Your Basket?' ":* (I) Tom O'Brien, San Francisco, 1976. This is a bogeyman story the informant learned from his English father around the turn of the century. For a close variant, see Briggs, *Dictionary,* vol. 1, p. 500. Also see Nuttall, *JAF* 8:122, for a reference to an ancient Mexican Indian tale of a human skull that chases passersby, stops when they stop, runs when they run.

4. OTHER DANGERS

p. 62 *"The Hook":* This legend is so well known, particularly on college campuses, that this telling is not based on any particular variant. For parallels, see Barnes, *SFQ* 30:310; Emrich, p. 333; Fouke, p. 263; Parochetti, *KFQ* 10:49; Thigpen, *IF* 4:183–86.

p. 65 *"The White Satin Evening Gown":* This tale has been reported in several sections of the United States, particularly the Midwest. The retelling is based on a number of variants. See Halpert, *HFB* 4:19–20, 32–34; Reaver, *NYFQ* 8:217–20.

p. 66 *"High Beams":* This retelling is based on a report by Carlos Drake in *IF* 1:107–109. For parallels, see Cord, *IF* 2:49–52; Parochetti, *KFQ* 10:47–49. In a variant I collected in Waverly, Iowa, a woman stops for gasoline at a service station in a rundown neighborhood. The attendant notices a man hiding in the back seat. He takes the woman's money, but does not return with her change. After waiting several minutes, she goes inside for her money. The attendant then tells her about the man, and she calls the police.

p. 69 *"The Babysitter":* (I) Jeff Rosen, sixteen, Jenkintown, Pennsylvania, 1980. In a widespread version, the intruder is captured by the police after the children are found murdered in their beds. The sitter escapes. See Fouke, p. 264. An American film based on this theme, *When a Stranger Calls,* was released in 1979.

5. "AAAAAAAAAAAH!"

p. 75 *"The Viper":* (I) Leslie Kush, fourteen, Philadelphia, 1980. For a parallel, see Knapp, p. 247.

p. 76 *"The Attic":* Compiler's recollection. In a variant, the hunter has two children who disappear. He decides to look for them in the attic, then screams when he opens the door. See Leach, *Rainbow,* pp. 218–19.

p. 78 *"The Slithery-Dee":* UMFA, (C) Andrea Lagoy; (I) Jackie Lagoy, Leominster, Massachusetts, 1972.

p. 81 *"Aaron Kelly's Bones":* This story is a retelling of a tale collected along the South Carolina coast prior to 1943. The collector was John Bennett. He reported the tale with the title "Daid Aaron II," in *The Doctor to the Dead,* pp. 249–52. His informants were Sarah Rutledge and Epsie Meggett, two black women who told the story in the Gullah dialect. Motif: E.410 (the unquiet grave).

p. 84 *"Wait till Martin Comes":* Retelling of a traditional Negro folk tale that has circulated in southeastern United States. In some versions the cat waits for "Emmett," "Patience," or "Whalem-Balem," instead of Martin. See Pucket, p. 132; Cox, *JAF* 47:352–55; Fauset, *JAF* 40:258–59; Botkin, *American,* p. 711.

p. 86 *"The Ghost with the Bloody Fingers":* WSFA, (C) Ramona Martin, 1973. In a variant, the ghost is a monster that kills everyone who occupies a haunted hotel room, except for a hippie who plays the guitar. See Vlach, *IF* 4:100–101.

Bibliography

Books

Books that may be of interest to young people are marked with an asterisk (*).

Beck, Horace P. *The Folklore of Maine.* Philadelphia: J. B. Lippincott Co., 1957.

Belden, Henry M. *Ballads and Songs Collected by the Missouri Folk-Lore Society,* vol. 15. Columbia, Mo.: University of Missouri, 1940.

Bennett, John. *The Doctor to the Dead: Grotesque Legends & Folk Tales of Old Charleston.* New York: Rinehart & Co., 1943.

Bett, Henry. *English Legends.* London: B. T. Batsford, 1952.

Blackwood, Algernon. "The Wendigo." In Basil Davenport, *Ghostly Stories to Be Told.* New York: Dodd, Mead & Co., 1950.

Blakeborough, Richard. *Wit, Character, Folklore & Customs of the North Riding of Yorkshire.* Salisbury-by-the-Sea, England: W. Rapp & Sons, 1911.

Bontemps, Arna, and Langston Hughes. *The Book of Negro Folklore.* New York: Dodd, Mead & Co., 1958.

Botkin, Benjamin A., ed. *A Treasury of American Folklore.* New York: Crown Publishers, 1944.

———, ed. *A Treasury of New England Folklore.* New York: Crown Publishers, 1965.

———, ed. *A Treasury of Southern Folklore.* New York: Crown Publishers, 1949.

Briggs, Katherine M. *A Dictionary of British Folk-Tales.* 4 vols. Bloomington, Ind.: Indiana University Press, 1967.

Brunvand, Jan H. *The Study of American Folklore.* 2nd ed. New York: W. W. Norton & Co., 1978.

———. *Urban American Legends.* New York: W. W. Norton & Co., 1980.

Burrison, John A. *"The Golden Arm": The Folk Tale and Its Literary Use by Mark Twain and Joel C. Harris.* Atlanta: Georgia State College School of Arts and Sciences Research Paper, 1968.

*Cerf, Bennett. *Famous Ghost Stories.* New York: Random House, 1944.

Chambers, Robert. *Popular Rhymes of Scotland.* London, Edinburgh: W. & R. Chambers, 1870. Reprint edition, Detroit: Singing Tree Press, 1969.

Chase, Richard, ed. *American Folk Tales and Songs.* New York: New American Library of World Literature, 1956. Reprint edition, New York: Dover Publications, 1971.

*———, ed. *Grandfather Tales.* Boston: Houghton Mifflin Co., 1948.

Cox, John H. *Folk-Songs of the South.* Cambridge, Mass.: Harvard University Press, 1925.

Creighton, Helen. *Bluenose Ghosts.* Toronto: Ryerson Press, 1957.

Dégh, Linda. "The 'Belief Legend' in Modern Society: Form, Function, and Relationship to Other Genres." In Wayland D. Hand, ed., *American Folk Legend, A Symposium.* Berkeley, Cal.: University of California Press, 1971.

Dorson, Richard M. *American Folklore.* Chicago: University of Chicago Press, 1959.

Flanders, Helen H., and George Brown. *Vermont Folk-Songs & Ballads.* Brattleboro, Vt.: Stephen Daye Press, 1932.

Fowke, Edith. *Folklore of Canada.* Toronto: McClelland and Stewart, 1976.

Gainer, Robert W. *Folklore of the Southern Appalachians.* Grantsville, W. Va.: Seneca Books, 1975.

Gardner, Emelyn E. *Folklore from the Schoharie Hills, New York.* Ann Arbor, Mich.: University of Michigan Press, 1937.

Halliwell-Phillips, James O. *The Nursery Rhymes of England.* London: Warne & Company, 1842.

Harris, Joel Chandler. *Nights With Uncle Remus: Myths and Legends of the Old Plantation.* Boston: Houghton Mifflin Co., 1882.

Hole, Christina. *Haunted England: A Survey of English Ghost-Lore.* London: B. T. Batsford, 1950.

*James, M. R. *The Collected Ghost Stories of M. R. James.* London: Edward Arnold & Co., 1931.

Johnson, Clifton. *What They Say in New England and Other American Folklore.* Boston: Lee and Shepherd, 1896. Reprint edition, Carl A. Withers, ed. New York: Columbia University Press, 1963.

Jones, Louis C. *Things That Go Bump in the Night.* New York: Hill and Wang, 1959.

Knapp, Mary and Herbert. *One Potato, Two Potato: The Secret Education of American Children.* New York: W. W. Norton & Co., 1976.

*Leach, Maria. *Rainbow Book of American Folk Tales and Legends.* Cleveland and New York: World Publishing Co., 1958.

———, ed. "Revenant." *Standard Dictionary of Folklore, Mythology and Legend.* New York: Funk & Wagnalls Publishing Co., 1972.

*———. *The Thing at the Foot of the Bed and Other Scary Stories.* Cleveland and New York: World Publishing Co., 1959.

*———. *Whistle in the Graveyard.* New York: The Viking Press, 1974.

Montell, William M. *Ghosts Along the Cumberland: Deathlore in the Kentucky Foothills.* Knoxville, Tenn.: University of Tennessee Press, 1975.

Musick, Ruth Ann. *The Telltale Lilac Bush and Other West Virginia Ghost Tales.* Lexington, Ky.: University of Kentucky Press, 1965.

Opie, Iona and Peter. *The Lore and Language of Schoolchildren.* Lon-

don: Oxford University Press, 1959.
———. *The Oxford Dictionary of Nursery Rhymes.* Oxford, England: Clarendon Press, 1951.
Puckett, Newbell N. *Folk Beliefs of the Southern Negro.* Chapel Hill, N.C.: University of North Carolina Press, 1926.
Randolph, Vance. *Ozark Folksongs.* Columbia, Mo.: State Historical Society of Missouri, 1949.
———. *Ozark Superstitions.* New York: Columbia University Press, 1947. Reprint edition, *Ozark Magic and Folklore.* New York: Dover Publications, 1964.
———. *Sticks in the Knapsack and Other Ozark Folk Tales.* New York: Columbia University Press, 1958.
———. *The Talking Turtle and Other Ozark Folk Tales.* New York: Columbia University Press, 1957.
Roberts, Leonard. *Old Greasybeard: Tales from the Cumberland Gap.* Detroit: Folklore Associates, 1969. Reprint edition, Pikeville, Ky.: Pikeville College Press, 1980.
———. *South from Hell-fer-Sartin: Kentucky Mountain Folk Tales.* Lexington, Ky.: University of Kentucky Press, 1955. Reprint edition, Pikeville, Ky.: Pikeville College Press, 1964.
———. *Up Cutshin and Down Greasy: The Couches' Tales and Songs.* Lexington, Ky.: University of Kentucky Press, 1959. Reprinted as *Sang Branch Settlers: Folksongs and Tales of an Eastern Kentucky Family,* Pikeville, Ky.: Pikeville College Press, 1980.
Sandburg, Carl. *The American Songbag.* New York: Harcourt, Brace & Co., 1927.
Shakespeare, William. *The Works of William Shakespeare.* New York: Oxford University Press, 1938.
White, Newman I. *American Negro Folk-Songs.* Cambridge, Mass.: Harvard University Press, 1928.

Articles

Bacon, A. M., and Parsons, E. C. "Folk-Lore from Elizabeth Cith County, Va." *JAF* 35 (1922):250–327.

Barnes, Daniel R. "Some Functional Horror Stories on the Kansas University Campus." *SFQ* 30 (1966):305–12.

Beardsley, Richard K., and Hankey, Rosalie. "The Vanishing Hitchhiker." *CFQ* 1 (1942):303–36.

———. "The History of the Vanishing Hitchhiker." *CFQ* 2 (1943):3–25.

Boggs, Ralph Steele. "North Carolina White Folktales and Riddles." *JAF* 47 (1934):289–328.

Brown, Jennifer. "The Cure and Feeding of Windigo: A Critique." *American Anthropologist* 73 (1971):20–21.

Cord, Xenia E. "Further Notes on 'The Assailant in the Back Seat.'" *IF* 2 (1969):50–54.

Cox, John H. "Negro Tales from West Virginia." *JAF* 47 (1934):341–57.

Crowe, Hume. "The Wendigo and the Bear Who Walks." *NMFR* 11 (1963–64):22–23.

Dégh, Linda. "The Hook and the Boy Friend's Death," *IF* 1 (1968):92–106.

Dorson, Richard. "The Folklore of Colleges." *The American Mercury* 68 (1949):671–77.

———. "The Runaway Grandmother." *IF* 1 (1968):68–69.

———. "The Roommate's Death and Related Dormitory Stories in Formation." *IF* 2 (1969):55–74.

Doyle, Charles Clay. "'As the Hearse Goes By': The Modern Child's *Memento Mori.*" PTFS 40 (1976):175–90.

Drake, Carlos. "The Killer in the Back Seat." *IF* 1 (1968):107–109.

Fauset, Arthur Huff. "Tales and Riddles Collected in Philadelphia." *JAF* 41 (1928):529–57.

Halpert, Herbert. "The Rash Dog and the Bloody Head." *HFB* 1 (1942):9–11.

Himelick, Raymond. "Classical Versions of 'The Poisoned Garment.'" *HF* 5 (1946):83–84.

Ives, Edward D. "The Haunted House and the Headless Ghost." *NEF* 4 (1962):61–67.

Jones, Louis C. "Hitchhiking Ghosts of New York." *CFQ* 4 (1945):284–92.

Kennedy, Ruth. "The Silver Toe." PTFS 6 (1927):41–42.

Nuttall, Zelia. "A Note on Ancient Mexican Folk-Lore." *JAF* 8 (1895):117–29.

Parochetti, JoAnn Stephens. "Scary Stories from Purdue." *KFQ* 10 (1965):49–57.

Parsons, Elsie Crews. "Tales from Guilford County, North Carolina." *JAF* 30 (1917):168–208.

Randolph, Vance. "Folk Tales from Arkansas." *JAF* 65 (1952):159–66.

Reaver, J. Russell. "'Embalmed Alive': A Developing Urban Ghost Tale." *NYFQ* 8 (1952):217–20.

Speck, Frank G. "Penobscot Tales and Religious Beliefs." *JAF* 48 (1935):1–107.

Stewart, Susan. "The Epistemology of the Scary Story." Scholarly article in process, 1980.

Stimson, Anna K. "Cries of Defiance and Derision, and Rhythmic Chants of West Side New York City (1893–1903)." *JAF* 58 (1945):124–29.

Theroux, Paul. "Christmas Ghosts." *The New York Times Book Review* (Dec. 23, 1979):1, 15.

Thigpen, Kenneth A., Jr. "Adolescent Legends in Brown County: A Survey." *IF* 4 (1971):183–207.

Vlach, John M. "One Black Eye and Other Horrors: A Case for the Humorous Anti-Legend." *IF* 4 (1971):95–124.

Acknowledgments

The following persons helped me to prepare this book:

Kendall Brewer, Frederick Seibert Brewer III, and Shawn Barry, who sat in the loft of a barn with me in Maine and told me scary stories.

The Boy Scouts at Camp Roosevelt at East Eddington, Maine, who told me their scary stories.

Several folklorists who shared with me their knowledge and scholarly resources, particularly Kenneth Goldstein of the University of Pennsylvania, Edward D. Ives of the University of Maine, and Susan Stewart of Temple University.

Other scholars whose articles and collections were important sources of information.

Librarians at the University of Maine (Orono), the University of Pennsylvania, Princeton University, and at the folklore archives listed on page 88.

My wife, Barbara, who did the musical notation in Chapters 1 and 3, carried out bibliographical research, and contributed in other ways.

I thank each of them.

A.S.

ALVIN SCHWARTZ is known for a body of work of more than two dozen books of folklore for young readers that explore everything from wordplay and humor to tales and legends of all kinds. His collections of scary stories—SCARY STORIES TO TELL IN THE DARK, MORE SCARY STORIES TO TELL IN THE DARK, SCARY STORIES 3, and two I Can Read Books, IN A DARK, DARK ROOM and GHOSTS!—are just one part of his matchless folklore collection.

STEPHEN GAMMELL's drawings have appeared in a number of books for children, including SCARY STORIES TO TELL IN THE DARK, MORE SCARY STORIES TO TELL IN THE DARK, and SCARY STORIES 3. He is the winner of the Caldecott Medal for his drawings in SONG AND DANCE MAN by Karen Ackerman. His art in WHERE THE BUFFALOES BEGIN by Olaf Baker earned him a Caldecott Honor, the *Boston Globe–Horn Book* Award, and a *New York Times* Best Illustrated Book citation. He also won a Caldecott Honor for his art in THE RELATIVES CAME by Cynthia Rylant. Mr. Gammell lives in St. Paul, Minnesota.

More Scary Stories to Tell in the Dark

· ALSO BY ALVIN SCHWARTZ ·

And the Green Grass Grew All Around
Folk Poetry from Everywhere

Chin Music
Talk Talk and Other Talk

Cross Your Fingers, Spit in Your Hat
Superstitions and Other Beliefs

Flapdoodle
Pure Nonsense from American Folklore

Kickle Snifters
and Other Fearsome Critters

Scary Stories to Tell in the Dark

Scary Stories 3
More Tales to Chill Your Bones

Stories to Tell a Cat

Telling Fortunes
Love Magic, Dream Signs, and Other Ways to Learn the Future

Tomfoolery
Trickery and Foolery with Words

A Twister of Twists, a Tangler of Tongues

Unriddling
All Sorts of Riddles to Puzzle Your Guessery,
Collected from American Folklore

When I Grew Up Long Ago
Older People Talk About the Days When They Were Young

Whoppers
Tall Tales and Other Lies

Witcracks
Jokes and Jests from American Folklore

· I Can Read Books® ·
(for younger readers)

All of Our Noses Are Here
and Other Noodle Tales

Buzy Buzzing Bumblebees
and Other Tongue Twisters

Ghosts!
Ghostly Tales from Folklore

I Saw You in the Bathtub
and Other Folk Rhymes

In a Dark, Dark Room
and Other Scary Stories

Ten Copycats in a Boat
and Other Riddles

There Is a Carrot in My Ear
and Other Noodle Tales

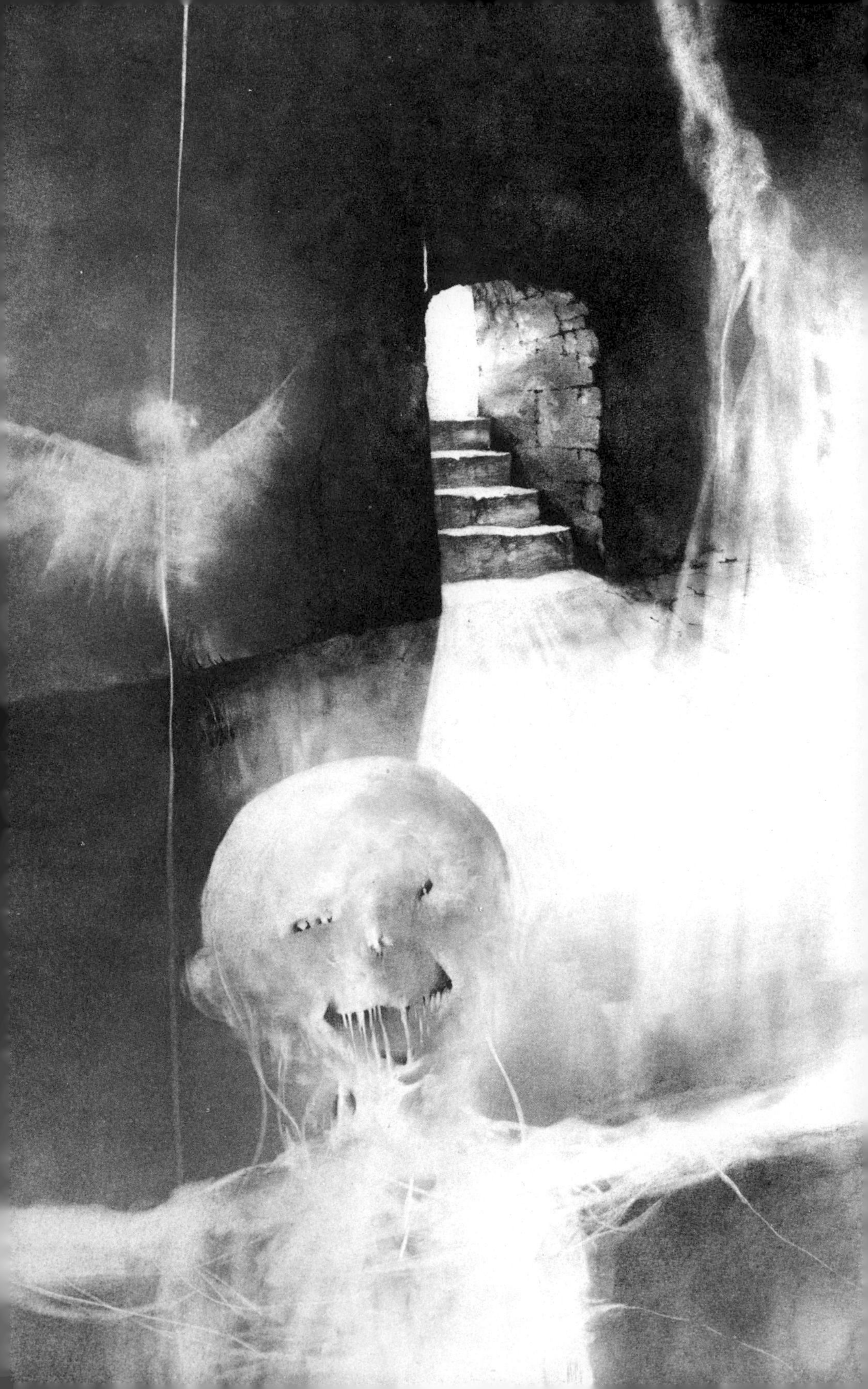

More Scary Stories to Tell in the Dark

Collected from Folklore and retold by

Alvin Schwartz

with drawings by Stephen Gammell

HarperCollins*Publishers*

 Printed in the United States of America. For information address HarperCollins Children's Books, a division of HarperCollins Publishers, 1350 Avenue of the Americas, New York, NY 10019.

Library of Congress-in-Publication Data
Schwartz, Alvin.
More scary stories to tell in the dark.
Sequel to: Scary stories to tell in the dark. 1981.
Bibliography: p.
Summary: More traditional and modern-day stories of ghosts, witches, vampires, "jump" stories, and scary songs.
ISBN 0-397-32081-7 — ISBN 0-397-32082-5 (lib. bdg.)
ISBN 0-06-440177-4 (pbk.)
1. Ghost stories, American. 2. Tales, American. [1. Ghosts—Fiction. 2. Horror stories. 3. Folklore—United States.] 1. Gammell, Stephen, ill. II. Title.
PZ8.1.S399Mo 1984 83-049494
398.2'5

Visit us on the World Wide Web!
www.harperchildrens.com

To Lauren

Acknowledgments

I am grateful to the girls and boys in many parts of the country who have shared with me their scary stories and told me about stories they would like to see in collections of this kind.

I am also grateful to the following persons and organizations for their generous help:

The librarians and library staff at the University of Maine (Orono), the University of Pennsylvania, Princeton University, and the Princeton, N.J., Public Library; Professor Edward D. Ives of the University of Maine and Professor Kenneth Goldstein of the University of Pennsylvania; my editors, Nina Ignatowicz and Robert O. Warren; and my wife and colleague, Barbara Carmer Schwartz.

A.S.

Contents

THE LAST LAUGH

Hoo-Ha's

These scary stories will take you on a strange and fearsome journey, where darkness or fog or mist or the sound of a person screaming or a dog howling turns ordinary places into nightmarish places, where nothing is what you expect.

People have been telling scary stories for as long as anyone knows. From the first, they were tales of supernatural creatures that people feared would harm them—bogeymen, monsters, demons, ghosts, and evil spirits lurking in the dark, waiting for a chance to strike.

We still tell stories about creatures we fear, but not all of them are about bogeymen and demons. Quite a few are about living people. You'll meet some of them—a fat and jolly butcher, a friendly girl who plays a drum, a neighbor, and others who, at best, are not to be trusted.

Scary stories of this kind often have a serious purpose. They may warn young people of dangers that await them when they set out in the world on their own.

But for the most part, we tell scary stories to have fun. We turn out the lights, or we leave just a candle burning. Then we sit close together and tell the scariest stories we know. Often these include some that have been passed down over hundreds of years.

If a story is scary enough, your flesh begins to creep. You get a shivery, shaky, screamy feeling. You imagine hearing and seeing things. You hold your breath as you wait to learn how it all ends. If something startling happens, everyone GASPS! or JUMPS! or SCREAMS!

Some people call those shivery, shaky, screamy feelings the "heebee jeebies" or the "screaming meemies." The poet T. S. Eliot called them the "hoo-ha's."

You'd better read the stories in this book while you are still feeling brave and *before* it gets dark. *Then,* when the moon is up, tell them to your friends and relatives. You'll probably give them the "hoo-ha's." But they'll have fun, and so will you.

Princeton, New Jersey — ALVIN SCHWARTZ

When She Saw Him, She Screamed and Ran

This chapter is filled with ghost stories. In one, a man has just become a ghost, but doesn't know it yet. In another, a pirate ship and crew return from a watery grave. And there are other frightful events.

· *SOMETHING WAS WRONG* ·

One morning John Sullivan found himself walking along a street downtown. He could not explain what he was doing there, or how he got there, or where he had been earlier. He didn't even know what time it was.

He saw a woman walking toward him and stopped her. "I'm afraid I forgot my watch," he said, and smiled. "Can you tell me the time?" When she saw him, she screamed and ran.

Then John Sullivan noticed that other people were afraid of him. When they saw him coming, they flattened themselves against a building, or ran across the street to stay out of his way.

"There must be something wrong with me," John Sullivan thought. "I'd better go home."

He hailed a taxi, but the driver took one look at him and sped away.

John Sullivan did not understand what was going on, and it scared him. "Maybe somebody at home can come and get me," he thought. He found a telephone and called his wife, but a voice he did not recognize answered.

"Is Mrs. Sullivan there?" he asked.

"No, she is at a funeral," the voice said. "Mr. Sullivan was killed yesterday in an accident downtown."

· *THE WRECK* ·

Fred and Jeanne went to the same high school, but they met for the first time at the Christmas dance. Fred had come by himself, and so had Jeanne. Soon Fred decided that Jeanne was one of the nicest girls he had ever met. They danced together most of the evening.

At eleven o'clock Jeanne said, "I have to leave now. Can you give me a ride?"

"Sure," he said. "I've got to go home, too."

"I accidentally drove my car into a tree on my way over here," Jeanne said. "I guess I wasn't paying attention."

Fred drove her to the head of Brady Road. It was in a neighborhood he didn't know very well.

"Why don't you drop me off here," Jeanne said. "The road up ahead is in really bad condition. I can walk from here."

Fred stopped the car and held out some tinsel. "Have some," he said. "I got it at the dance."

"Thank you," she said. "I'll put it in my hair," and she did.

"Would you like to go out sometime, to a movie or something?" Fred asked.

"That would be fun," Jeanne said.

After Fred drove off, he realized that he did not know Jeanne's last name or her telephone number. "I'll go back," he thought. "The road can't be that bad."

He drove slowly down Brady Road through a thick woods, but there wasn't a sign of Jeanne. As he came around a curve, he saw the wreckage of a car ahead. It had crashed into a tree and had caught fire. Smoke was still rising from it.

As Fred made his way to the car, he could see someone trapped inside, crushed against the steering column.

It was Jeanne. In her hair was the Christmas tinsel he had given her.

· ONE SUNDAY MORNING ·

Ida always went to the seven o'clock Sunday morning service at her church. Usually she heard the clanging of the church bells while she was eating breakfast. But this morning she heard them while she was still in bed.

"That means I'm late," she thought.

Ida jumped out of bed, quickly dressed and left without eating or looking at the clock. It was still dark outside, but it usually was dark at this time of year. Ida was the only one on the street. The only sounds she heard were the clatter of her shoes on the pavement. "Everybody must already be in church," she thought.

Ida took a short cut through the cemetery, then she quietly slipped into the church and found a seat. The service had already begun.

When she caught her breath, Ida looked around. The church was filled with people she had never seen before. But the woman next to her did look familiar. Ida smiled at her. "It's Josephine Kerr," she thought. "But she's dead! She died a month ago." Suddenly Ida felt uneasy.

She looked around again. As her eyes began to adjust to the dim light, Ida saw some skeletons in suits and dresses. "This is a service for the dead," Ida thought. "Everybody here is dead, except me."

Ida noticed that some of them were staring at her. They looked angry, as if she had no business there. Josephine Kerr leaned toward her and whispered, "Leave right after the benediction, if you care for your life."

When the service came to an end, the minister gave his blessing. "The Lord bless you and keep you," he said. "The Lord make his face to shine upon you . . ."

Ida grabbed her coat and walked quickly toward the door. When she heard footsteps behind her, she glanced back. Several of the dead were coming toward her. Others were getting up to join them.

"The Lord lift up his countenance to you . . ." the minister went on.

Ida was so frightened she began to run. Out the door she ran, with a pack of shrieking ghosts at her heels.

"Get out!" one of them screamed. Another shouted, "You don't belong here!" and ripped her coat away. As Ida ran through the cemetery, a third grabbed the hat from her head. "Don't come back!" it screamed, and shook its arm at her.

By the time Ida reached the street, the sun was rising, and the dead had disappeared.

"Did this really happen?" Ida asked herself, "or have I been dreaming?"

That afternoon one of Ida's friends brought over her coat and hat, or what was left of them. They had been found in the cemetery, torn to shreds.

· *SOUNDS* ·

The house was near the beach. It was a big old place where nobody had lived for years. From time to time somebody would force open a window or a door and spend the night there. But never longer.

Three fishermen caught in a storm took shelter there one night. With some dry wood they found inside, they made a fire in the fireplace. They lay down on the floor and tried to get some sleep, but none of them slept that night.

First they heard footsteps upstairs. It sounded like there were several people moving back and forth, back and forth. When one of the fishermen called, "Who's up there?" the footsteps stopped. Then they heard a woman scream. The scream turned into a groan and died away. Blood began to drip from the ceiling into the room where the fishermen huddled. A small red pool formed on the floor and soaked into the wood.

A door upstairs crashed shut, and again the woman screamed. "Not me!" she cried. It sounded as if she was running, her high heels tapping wildly down the hall. "I'll get you!" a man shouted, and the floor shook as he chased her.

Then silence. There wasn't a sound until the man who had shouted began to laugh. Long peals of horrible laughter filled the house. It went on and on until the fishermen thought they would go mad.

When finally it stopped, the fishermen heard someone coming down the stairs dragging something heavy that bumped on each step. They heard him drag it through the front hall and out the front door. The door opened; then it slammed shut. Again, silence.

Suddenly a flash of lightning filled the house with a green blaze of light. A ghastly face stared at the fishermen from the hallway. Then came a crash of thunder. Terrified, they ran out into the storm.

· A WEIRD BLUE LIGHT ·

Late one night in October, 1864, a Confederate blockade runner slipped by some Union gunboats at the entrance to Galveston Bay in Texas and made it safely to port with its cargo of food and other necessities.

Louis Billings, the master of the small vessel, was getting ready to weigh anchor when he was startled by a shriek from one of the crew.

"A strange, old-fashioned schooner with a big black flag was rushing down at us," Billings said later. "She was afire with a sort of weird, pale-blue light that lighted up every nook and cranny of her.

"The crew was pulling at the ropes and doing other work, and they paid us no attention, didn't even glance our way. They all had ghastly bleeding wounds, but their faces and eyes were those of dead men.

"The man who had shrieked had fallen to his knees, his teeth chattering as he gasped out a prayer. Overcoming my own terror, that was chilling the very marrow of my bones, I rushed forward, shouting to the others as I ran. Suddenly the schooner vanished before my eyes."

Some say that it was the ghost of Jean Lafitte's pirate ship *Pride* that sank off Galveston Island in 1821 or 1822. She was seen again in 1892 in the same waters with the same crew.

· *SOMEBODY FELL FROM ALOFT* ·

I had signed on as an ordinary seaman on the *Falls of Ettrick,* a merchant ship bound for England. The first time I saw that ship, I knew her right away. She was the old *Gertrude Spurshoe.* I had sailed on her years before when she was painted brown and gold. Now she was painted black and had a new name, but it was the same ship for sure.

We had a pretty good crew for that voyage, except for one hard-looking ticket named McLaren. He was a pretty good seaman, but there was something about him that I didn't trust. He was kind of secretive. Kept mostly to himself.

One day somebody told him that I had worked on the old *Gertrude.* For some reason he got all a-tremble over that. Then I ketched him giving me all of these ugly black looks, as if he was itchin' to knife me in the back. I guessed it had something to do with the *Gertrude,* but I didn't know what.

Well, this one day we was tryin' to work our way through a drippin' black fog. You'd scarcely know we had all the lights on. And it was dead calm. There wasn't a breath of fresh air. The ship just lay there wallowing in a trough, a-rollin' and a-rollin', goin' nowheres.

I was standing my watch around midships, and McLaren was doin' his trick at the wheel. The rest of the crew was scattered around one place and another. It was as quiet as could be.

Then all at once—WHACKO! This thing hits the deck right in front of McLaren! He lets go a screech that turns my blood cold and he falls down in a faint.

The second mate starts yellin' that somebody has fallen from aloft. Layin' out there just forward of the wheel was someone, or something, dressed in oilskins with blood oozin' out from underneath. The captain ran and fetched a big light from his cabin so we could see who it was.

They kind of straightened him out to get a good look at his face. He was a big, ugly-lookin' devil. But nobody knew who he was or what he was doin' up there. At least nobody was sayin'.

When McLaren came to from his faint, they tried to get somethin' out of him. All he did was jabber away and keep rollin' those big, wild-looking eyes of his.

Everybody was gettin' more and more excited. We all wanted to heave the body overboard as quick as we could. There was somethin' weird about it, as if it wasn't real.

But the captain wasn't so sure about getting rid of it that way. "Could it be a stowaway?" he asked. But the ship was so filled with lumber we were carryin', there was no space where a livin' thing could hide for three weeks, which is how long we had been out. Even if it was a stowaway, what was it doing aloft on such a dirty day? There was no reason for anyone to be up there. There was nothin' to see.

Finally, the captain gave up and told us to heave him overboard. Then nobody would touch him. The mate ordered us to pick him up, but nobody made a move. Then he tried coaxin', but that didn't do any good.

Suddenly that loony McLaren starts yellin', "I handled him once, and I can handle him again!" He picks up the body, and staggers over to the railin' with it. He is just about to throw it overboard when it wraps its two big, long arms around him, and over they go together! Then on the way down, one of them starts laughin' in a horrible way.

The mates are yellin' to launch a boat, but nobody would get into a boat, not on a night like that. We threw a couple of life preservers after them, but everybody knew they wouldn't help. So that was that. Or was it?

The first chance I had to go home after that, I went right over to see old Captain Spurshoe, who was captain when the *Gertrude* was around.

"Well," he says, "one trip these two outlandish men shipped aboard the *Gertrude.* One was McLaren, the other was a really big fella. The big one was always pickin' on McLaren and thumpin' him around. And McLaren was always talkin' about how he would get back at him.

"Well, this wet, dirty night the two of them was up there alone, and the big one come flyin' down, killed himself deader'n a herring.

"McLaren says the foot rope they were using parted and how he almost fell himself. But everybody who saw that rope knew she didn't give away on her own. She had been cut through with a knife.

"After that whenever we came into port, McLaren thought we were goin' to get the police after him, and he'd get pretty scared. But we couldn't prove anything, so we didn't try. In the end, I guess the big fella took care of things in his own way. If he was a ghost that came back, that's what he was—if there be things like ghosts."

· THE LITTLE BLACK DOG ·

Billy Mansfield said that a little black dog followed him wherever he went. But he was the only one who saw it. So people thought he was kind of crazy. To drive the dog away, Billy was always hollering at it, throwing rocks at it. But the dog always came back.

The first time Billy saw that dog was the day he fought Silas Burton. Billy was just a young man then, but the Burtons and Billy's family had been feuding for years.

When Billy saw Silas riding toward him, he went for his gun and Burton went for his. But Billy fired first. He hit Burton in the back, knocking him from his horse. Burton's horse ran off, and his gun fell where he couldn't reach it.

He lay there on the ground pleading with Billy not

to kill him, but Billy killed him anyway. Burton's little black dog was with him when he was shot. The dog kept licking Burton's face, and barking and snarling at Billy. In his anger, Billy killed the dog too.

There wasn't much law enforcement in those days, so Billy wasn't arrested. But all that night he heard Burton's dog outside his cabin, scratching on his door and barking to be let in. "I'm imagining this," Billy said to himself. "I shot that dog. It's dead."

But the next morning Billy *saw* the dog. It was waiting for him outside. From then on there was not a day when he didn't see it. And there wasn't a night when he didn't hear it scratching on his door, barking to be let in.

From then on, Billy was always finding black dog hairs on the sofa, on the floor, in his bed, even in his food. And the house and the yard stank of dog. That's what Billy said.

Whenever somebody told him there wasn't any dog to see, he'd say, "Maybe *you* don't see it, but I do. And I'm not any crazier than you are."

Things went on like that for many years. Then one morning in the middle of the winter the neighbors didn't see any smoke coming out of Billy's chimney. When they went over to check, Billy wasn't there. A day or so later they found his body lying in the snow in a field back of his cabin.

Billy had plenty of enemies, and at first it seemed like somebody might have killed him. But there wasn't a mark on his body. And there weren't any footprints out there, except for Billy's.

The doctor said Billy probably died of old age. But there was something odd about his death. When the neighbors found Billy, there were black dog hairs on his clothes. There were even a few on his face. It smelled like a dog had been out there. Yet no one had seen a dog anywhere.

· CLINKITY-CLINK ·

An old lady got sick and died. She had no family and no close friends. So the neighbors got a gravedigger to dig a grave for her. And they had a coffin made, and they placed it in her living room. As was the tradition, they washed her body and dressed her up in her best clothes and put her in the coffin.

When she died her eyes were wide open, staring at everything and seeing nothing. The neighbors found two old silver dollars on her dresser, and they put them on her eyelids to keep them closed.

They lit candles and sat up with her so that she would not be too lonely on that first night that she was dead. The next morning a preacher came and said a prayer for her. Then everybody went home.

Later the gravedigger arrived to take her to the cemetery and bury her. He stared at the silver dollars on her eyes, and he picked them up. How shiny and smooth they were! How thick and heavy! "They're beautiful," he thought, "just beautiful."

He looked at the dead woman. With her eyes wide open, he felt she was staring at him, watching him hold her coins. It gave him a creepy feeling. He put the coins back on those eyes of hers to keep them closed.

But before he knew it, his hands reached out again and grabbed the coins and stuck them in his pocket.

Then he grabbed a hammer and quickly nailed shut the lid on the coffin.

"Now you can't see anything!" he said to her. Then he took her out to the cemetery, and he buried her as fast as he could.

When the gravedigger got home, he put the two silver dollars in a tin box and shook it. The coins made a cheerful rattling sound, but the gravedigger wasn't feeling cheerful. He couldn't forget those eyes looking at him.

When it got dark, a storm came up, and the wind started blowing. It blew all around the house. It came in through the cracks and around the windows, and down the chimney.

BUZ-OOOOOO-O-O-O! it went. *Bizee, bizee, BUZ-OOOOOO-O-O-O!* The fire flared and flickered.

The gravedigger threw some fresh wood on the fire, got into bed, and pulled the blankets up to his chin.

The wind kept blowing. *BUZ-OOOOOO-O-O-O!* it went. *Bizee, bizee, BUZ-OOOOOO-O-O-O!* The fire flared and flickered and cast evil-looking shadows on the walls.

The gravedigger lay there thinking about the dead woman's eyes staring at him. The wind blew stronger and louder, and the fire flared and flickered, and popped and snapped, and he got more and more scared.

Suddenly he heard another sound. *Clinkity-clink, clinkity-clink,* it went. *Clinkity-clink, clinkity-clink.* It was the silver dollars rattling in the tin box.

"Hey!" the gravedigger shouted. "Who's taking my money?"

But all he heard was the wind blowing, *Bizee, bizee, BUZ-OOOOOO-O-O-O!* and the flames flaring and flickering, and snapping and popping, and the coins going *Clinkity-clink, clinkity-clink.*

He leaped out of bed and chained up the door. Then he hurried back. But his head had barely touched the pillow when he heard, *Clinkity-clink, clinkity-clink.*

Then he heard something way off in the distance. It was a voice crying, "Where is my money? Who's got my money? Whoooo? Whoooo?"

And the wind blew *Bizee, bizee, BUZ-OOOOOO-O-O-O!* And the fire flared and flickered and snapped and popped, and the money went *Clinkity-clink, clinkity-clink.*

The gravedigger was really scared. He got out of bed again and piled all the furniture against the door, and he put a heavy iron skillet over the tin box. Then he jumped back into bed and covered his head with the blankets.

But the money rattled louder than ever, and way off a voice cried, "Give me my money! Who's got my money! Whoooo? Whoooo?" And the wind blew and the fire flared and flickered and snapped and popped, and the gravedigger shivered and shook and cried, "Oh, Lordy, Lordy!"

Suddenly the front door flew open, and in walked the ghost of the dead woman with her eyes wide open, staring at everything and seeing nothing. And the wind blew *Bizee, bizee, BUZ-OOOOOO-O-O-O!* and the money went *Clinkity-clink, clinkity-clink,* and the fire flared and flickered and snapped and popped, and the ghost of the dead woman cried, "Oh, where is my money? Who's got my money? Whoooo? Whoooo?" And the grave-digger moaned, "Oh, Lordy, Lordy!"

The ghost could hear her money going *Clinkity-clink, clinkity-clink,* in the tin box. But her dead eyes couldn't see the box. So she reached out with her arms and tried to find it.

(As you tell the story, stand up with your arms in front of you and begin groping around you.)

The wind went *Bizee, bizee, BUZ-OOOOOO-O-O-O!* and the money rattled, *Clinkity-clink, clinkity-clink!* and the fire flared and flickered and snapped and popped, and the gravedigger shivered and shook and moaned, "Oh, Lordy, Lordy!" And the woman cried, "Give me my money! Who's got my money? Whoooo? Whoooo?"

(Now quickly jump at somebody in the audience and scream:)

YOU'VE GOT IT!

She Was Spittin' and Yowlin' Just Like a Cat

The tales in this chapter are about an empty trunk, a neighbor who turns into a cat, a strange drum, some very tasty sausages, and other scary things.

· *THE BRIDE* ·

The minister's daughter had just gotten married. After the wedding ceremony there was a great feast, with music and dancing and contests and games, even old children's games.

When they got to playing hide-and-seek, the bride decided to hide in her grandfather's trunk up in the attic.

"They'll never find me there," she thought.

As she was climbing into the trunk, the lid came down and cracked her on the head, and she fell unconscious inside. The lid slammed shut and locked.

No one will ever know how long she called for help or how hard she struggled to free herself from that tomb. Everyone in the village searched for her, and they looked almost everywhere. But no one thought of looking in the trunk. After a week her brand-new bridegroom and all the others gave her up for lost.

Years later a maid went up into the attic looking for something she needed. "Maybe it is in the trunk," she thought. She opened it—and screamed. There lay the missing bride in her wedding dress, but by then she was only a skeleton.

· *RINGS ON HER FINGERS* ·

Daisy Clark had been in a coma for more than a month when the doctor said that she had finally died. She was buried on a cool summer day in a small cemetery about a mile from her home.

"May she always rest in such peace," her husband said.

But she didn't. Late that night a grave robber with a shovel and a lantern began to dig her up. Since the ground was still soft, he quickly reached the coffin and got it open.

His hunch was right. Daisy had been buried wearing

two valuable rings—a wedding ring with a diamond in it, and a ring with a ruby that glowed as if it were alive.

The thief got down on his knees and reached into the coffin to get the rings. But they were stuck fast on her fingers. So he decided that the only way to get them was to cut off her fingers with a knife.

But when he cut into the finger with the wedding ring, it began to bleed, and Daisy Clark began to stir. Suddenly she sat up! Terrified, the thief scrambled to his feet. He accidentally kicked over the lantern, and the light went out.

He could hear Daisy climb out of her grave. As she moved past him in the dark, he stood there frozen with fear, clutching the knife in his hand.

When Daisy saw him, she pulled her shroud around her and asked, "Who are you?" When the grave robber heard this "corpse" speak, he ran! Daisy shrugged her shoulders and walked on, and never once looked back.

But in his fear and confusion, the thief fled in the wrong direction. He pitched headlong into her grave, fell on the knife, and stabbed himself. While Daisy walked home, the thief bled to death.

· *THE DRUM* ·

Once there were two sisters. Dolores was seven, and Sandra was five. They lived in a small house in the country with their mother and their baby brother, Arthur. Their father was a seaman and was away on a long voyage.

One day Dolores and Sandra were running across a field near their house when they met a gypsy girl playing a drum. Her family was camping in the field for a few days.

As the girl played, a little mechanical man and woman came out of the drum and danced. Dolores and Sandra had never seen such a drum, and they begged the girl to give it to them.

She looked at them and laughed. "I will give it to you," she said, "but only if you are really bad. Come back tomorrow and tell me how bad you were, and I will see."

As soon as the two sisters got home, they started shouting, which was against the rules in their house. Then they wrote all over the walls with their crayons. At supper, they spilled their food. And when it was time for bed, they wouldn't go. They did everything they could think of to upset their mother. They were really bad.

Early the next morning, they hurried off to find the

gypsy girl. "We were really bad yesterday," they told her, "so please give us the drum."

But when they told her what they had done, the gypsy girl laughed.

"Oh, you must be much worse than *that* if I am to give you the drum," she said.

As soon as Dolores and Sandra got home, they pulled up all the flowers in the garden. They let the pig out, and chased it away. They tore their clothes. They sloshed in the mud. They were a lot worse than the day before.

"If you do not stop," their mother said, "I will go away and take Arthur with me. And you will get a new mother with glass eyes and a wooden tail."

That scared Dolores and Sandra. They loved their mother, and they loved Arthur. They could not imagine being without them, and they began to cry.

"I don't want to leave you," their mother said. "But unless you change your behavior, I will have to leave you."

"We'll be good," the girls promised. Yet they did not really believe that their mother would go away.

"She is just trying to scare us," Dolores said later.

"We'll get the drum tomorrow," said Sandra. "Then we'll be good again."

Early the next morning, they rushed off to find the gypsy girl. When they found her, she was playing the drum again, and the little man and woman were dancing.

They told the gypsy girl how bad they had been the day before. "That must be bad enough to get the drum," they said.

"Oh, no," said the gypsy girl. "You must be *much* worse than that."

"But we promised our mother to be good from now on," said the girls.

"If you really want the drum," said the gypsy girl, "you must be much worse."

"It's only for one more day," Dolores told Sandra. "Then we will have the drum."

"I hope you're right," Sandra said.

As soon as they got home, they beat the dog with a stick. They broke the dishes. They tore their clothes to pieces. They spanked their baby brother Arthur.

Their mother began to cry. "You are not keeping your promise," she said.

"We will be good," said Dolores.

"We promise," said Sandra.

"I can't wait much longer," said their mother. "Please try."

Early the next morning, before their mother was awake, Dolores and Sandra ran to see the gypsy girl. They told her all about the bad things they had done the day before.

"We were horrid," said Sandra.

"We were worse than we have ever been," said Dolores. "Can we have the drum now, please?"

"No," said the gypsy girl. "I never meant to give it to you. It was just a game we were playing. I thought you knew that."

Dolores and Sandra began to cry. They rushed home as quickly as they could. But their mother and Arthur were gone. "They are out shopping," said Dolores.

"They'll be back soon." But they were still not back when time for lunch came.

Dolores and Sandra felt lonely and scared. They wandered through the fields the rest of the day. "Maybe they will be home when we get back," said Dolores.

When they got home, they saw through the window that the lamps were lit, and there was a fire in the fireplace. But they did not see their mother and Arthur. Instead, there was their new mother—her glass eyes glistening, her wooden tail thumping on the floor.

· THE WINDOW ·

Margaret and her brothers, Paul and David, shared a small house on top of a hill just outside the village.

It was so warm one summer's night that Margaret could not sleep. She sat up in bed in the darkness of her room watching the moon move across the sky. Suddenly something caught her eye.

She saw two small yellow-green lights moving through the woods near the graveyard at the bottom of the hill. They looked like the eyes of some animal. But she could not make out what kind of a creature it was.

Soon the creature left the woods and moved up the hill toward the house. For a few minutes, Margaret lost sight of it. Then she saw it coming across the lawn toward her window. It looked something like a man, and yet it didn't.

Margaret was terrified. She wanted to run from her room. But the door was next to her window. She was afraid the creature would see her and break in before she could escape.

When the creature turned and moved in another direction, Margaret rushed to the door. But before she could open the door, it was back. Margaret found herself staring through the window at a shrunken face like that of a mummy. Its yellow-green eyes gleamed like a cat's eyes. She wanted to scream, but she was so frightened that she could not make a sound.

The creature broke the window glass, unlocked the window, and crawled inside. Margaret tried to flee, but the creature caught her. It twisted its long, bony fingers into her hair, pulled back her head, and sank its teeth into her throat.

Margaret screamed, and fainted. When her brothers heard her piercing scream, they rushed to her room. But by the time they got the door unlocked, the creature had fled. Margaret lay on the floor bleeding and unconscious. While Paul tried to stop the bleeding, David chased the creature down the hill toward the graveyard. But soon he lost sight of it.

The police thought it was the work of an escaped lunatic who believed he was a vampire.

When Margaret recovered, her brothers wanted to move to a safer place where it would be harder to break in. But Margaret refused. The creature would never come back. She was sure of that. But just in case, Paul and David began to keep loaded pistols in their rooms.

One night months later, Margaret was awakened by a scratching sound at the window. When she opened her eyes, there was the same shrunken face staring in at her.

That night her brothers heard her cries in time. They chased the creature down the hill, and David shot it in the leg. But the creature managed to scramble over the graveyard wall and disappeared near an old burial vault.

The next day, Margaret and her brothers watched as the sexton of the church opened the burial vault. Inside was a horrifying scene—broken coffins, bones, and rotting flesh were scattered all over the floor.

Only one coffin had not been disturbed. When the sexton opened it, there lay the creature with the shrunken face that had attacked Margaret. The telltale bullet was in its leg.

They did the only thing they knew of to rid themselves of a vampire. The sexton built a roaring blaze outside the vault, and fed the shrunken body to the flames. They watched the body burn until nothing remained but ashes.

· *WONDERFUL SAUSAGE* ·

One dark, rainy Saturday afternoon, a fat and jolly butcher named Samuel Blunt had an argument over money with his wife, Eloise. Blunt lost his temper and killed Eloise. Then he ground her up into sausage meat and buried her bones under a big flat rock in the backyard. To keep the murder a secret, he told everyone that she had moved away.

Blunt mixed his new sausage meat with pork, then seasoned it with salt and pepper, added some sage and thyme and a bit of garlic. To give it a special flavor, he smoked it in his smokehouse for a while. He called it "Blunt's Special Sausage."

There was such a demand for this new sausage that Blunt bought the best hogs he could find and started raising his own pork. He also kept a sharp lookout for humans who might make a tasty sausage meat.

One day a nice, plump schoolteacher came into his shop. Blunt grabbed her and ground her up. Another time Blunt's dentist came by. He was a little, round man, and into the grinder he went. Then one by one, the children in the neighborhood began to disappear. And so did their kittens and puppies. But no one ever dreamed that Blunt the butcher had anything to do with it.

Things went on that way for years. Then one day Blunt made a big mistake. A fat boy came into the butcher shop. Blunt grabbed him and started to drag him off to the sausage grinder. But the boy broke loose, and ran out of the shop, and Blunt chased after him waving a big butcher knife.

When people saw this, they realized at once what had become of all the missing children and grown-ups and kittens and puppies. An angry crowd gathered at the butcher shop. No one knows for sure just what happened to Blunt that day. Some say he was fed to his hogs. Others say he was fed to his sausage grinder. But he was never seen again, and neither was his wonderful sausage meat.

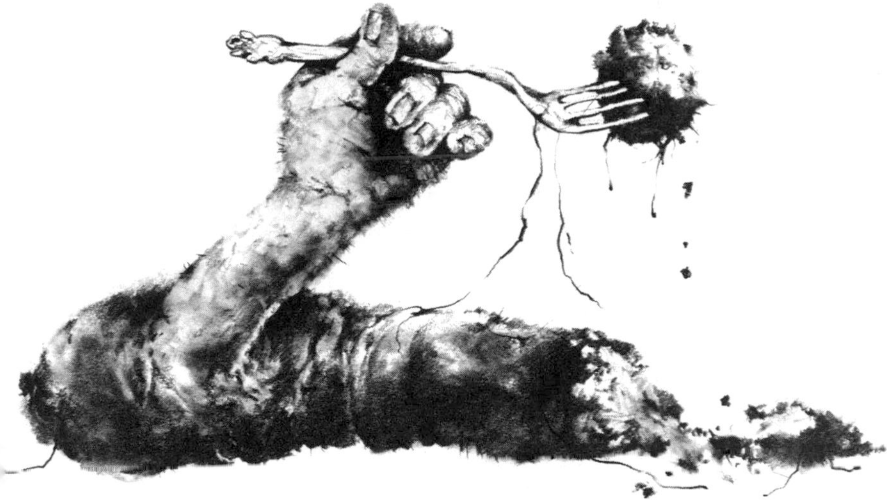

· *THE CAT'S PAW* ·

Somebody was stealing the meat Jed Smith kept in his smokehouse. Every day a ham, or some bacon, or something else was missing. Finally, Jed decided he had to put a stop to it. One night he hid in the smokehouse with his rifle and waited for the thief.

He didn't have to wait long, for soon a black she-cat slunk in. She was the biggest cat Jed had ever seen. When she jumped up and pulled down a ham hanging from the ceiling, Jed grabbed his rifle and turned on the lights. But instead of running away, the cat jumped at him. He fired, and shot off one of her paws.

Jed was sure he heard a woman scream right after his gun went off. The cat began tearing around the room, spitting and yowling. Then she ran up the chimney and was gone.

Jed stared at the cat's paw. Only it wasn't a cat's paw anymore. A woman's foot lay wriggling on the floor, all shot up and bloody.

"So it's a witch that's been doing it," he told himself.

Just then one of Jed's neighbors, a fellow named Burdick, came racing down the road to get a doctor. His wife's foot had been shot in an accident, he told Jed. "She's bleedin' pretty bad," he said.

The doctor got to her barely in time. People who were there when it happened said that she was "spittin' and yowlin' just like a cat."

· *THE VOICE* ·

Ellen had just fallen asleep when she heard a strange voice.

"Ellen," it whispered, *"I am coming up the stairs.*

"I am on the first step.

"Now I am on the second step."

Ellen got scared and called her parents, but they didn't hear her, and they didn't come.

Then the voice whispered, *"Ellen, I'm on the top step.*

"Now I'm in the hall.

"Now I'm outside your room."

Then it whispered, *"I'm standing right next to your bed."*

And then,

"I'VE GOT YOU!"

Ellen screamed, and the voice stopped. Her father rushed into the room and turned on the light.

"Somebody is in here!" Ellen said. They looked and looked. Nobody was there.

When I Wake Up, Everything Will Be All Right

There are scary stories here about a subway car, a shopping mall, and other dangerous places.

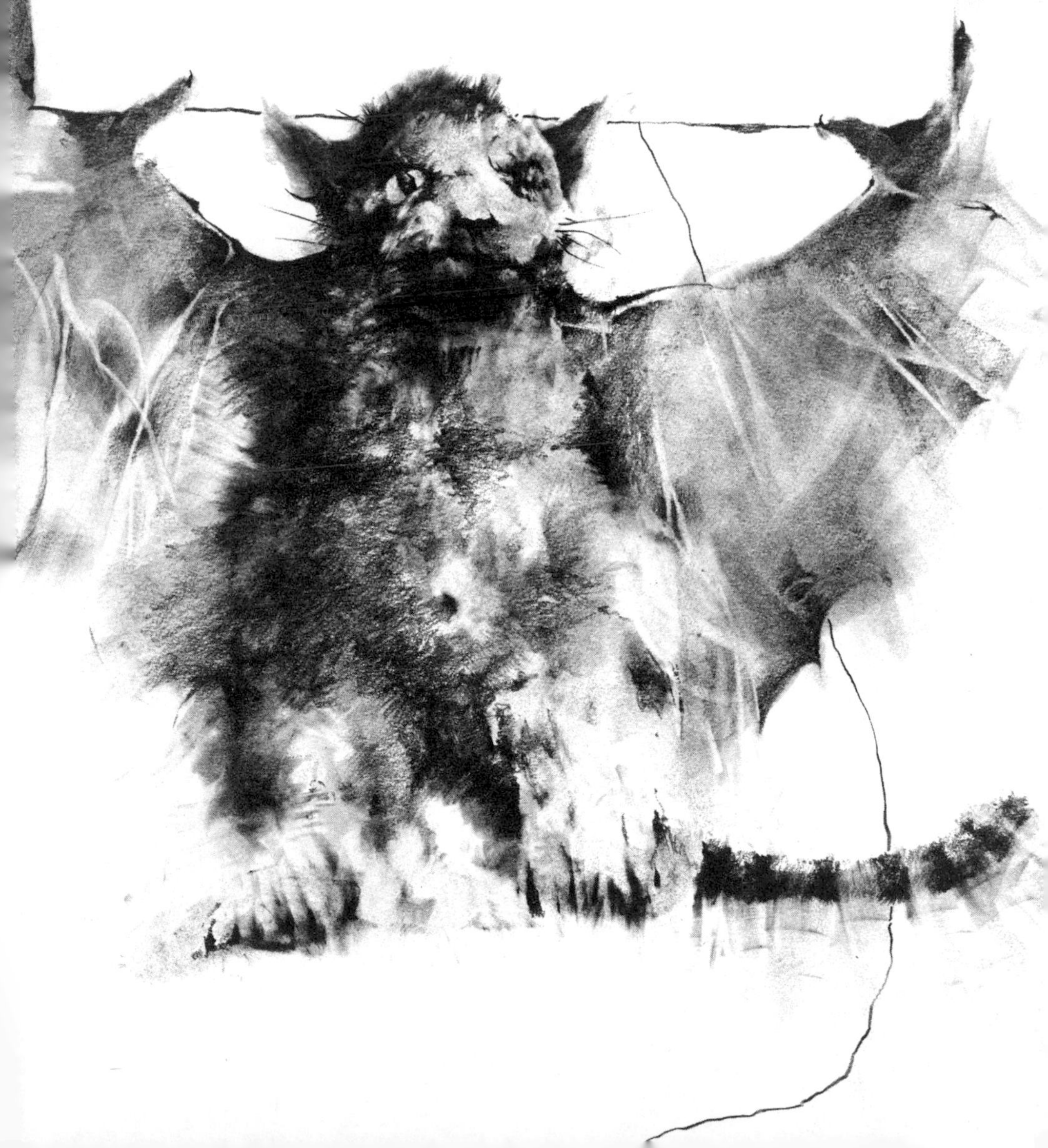

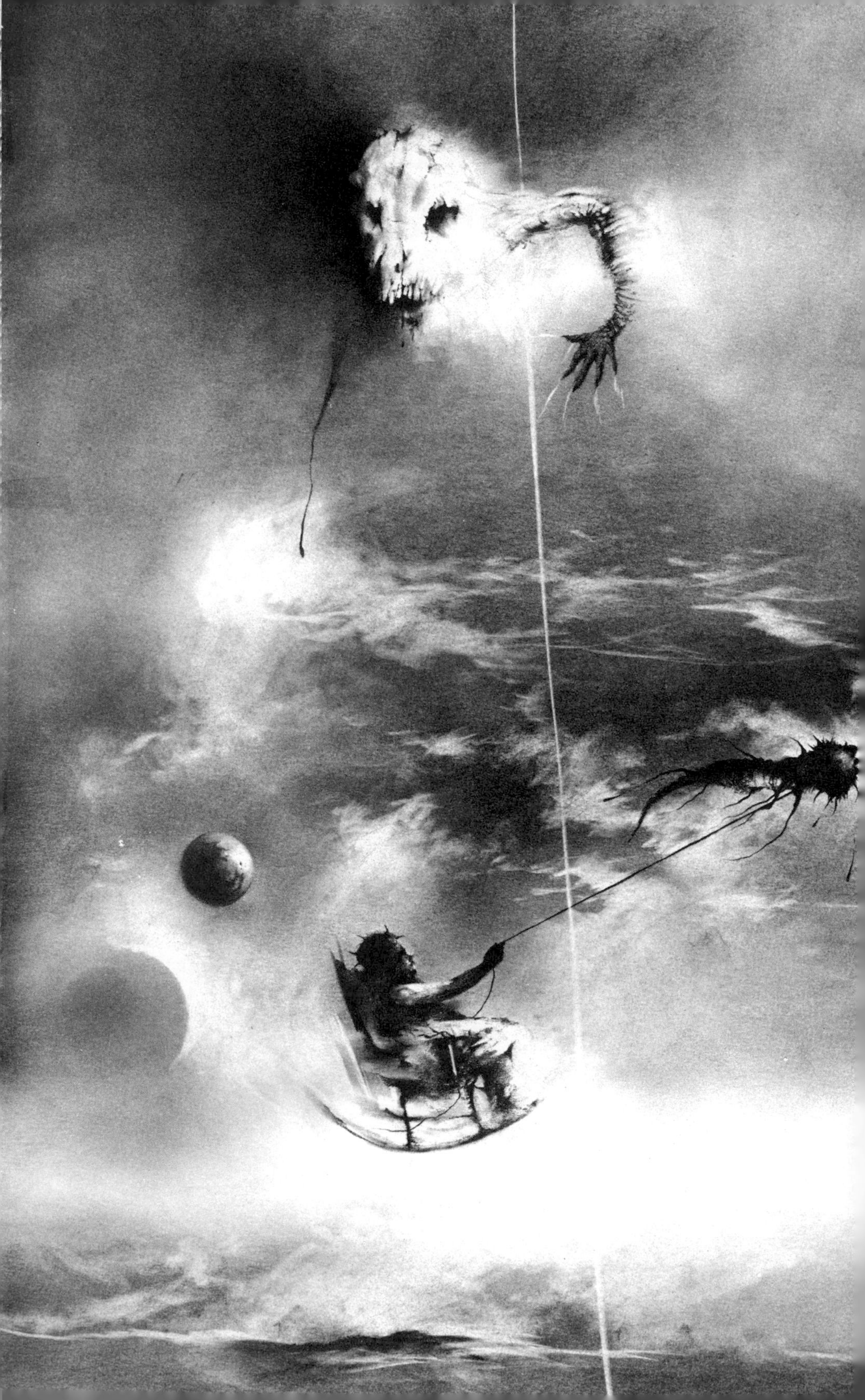

· "OH, SUSANNAH!" ·

Susannah and Jane shared a small apartment near the university where they were students. When Susannah got back from the library one night, the lights were out and Jane was asleep. Susannah undressed in the dark and quietly got into bed.

She had almost fallen asleep when she heard someone humming the tune to the song "Oh, Susannah!"

"Jane," she said, "please stop humming; I want to get some sleep."

Jane didn't answer, but the humming stopped, and Susannah fell asleep. She awakened early the next morning—too early, she decided—and was trying to get back to sleep when she heard the humming again.

"Please go back to sleep," she told Jane. "It's too early to get up."

Jane didn't answer, but the humming continued. Susannah became angry. "Cut it out!" she said. "It's not funny." When the humming still did not stop, she lost her temper. She jumped out of bed, pulled the covers off Jane, and screamed. . . .

Jane's head was gone! Somebody had cut off her head!

"I'm having a nightmare," Susannah told herself. "When I wake up, everything will be all right. . . ."

· *THE MAN IN THE MIDDLE* ·

It was almost midnight. Sally Truitt had just gotten on the subway train at Fiftieth Street after visiting her mother.

"Don't worry," Sally had told her. "The subway is safe. There is always a policeman on duty." But that night she didn't see one. Except for her, the subway car was empty.

At Forty-second Street, three tough-looking men got on. Two of them were holding up the third, who looked drunk. His head rolled from side to side, and his legs refused to work.

When they got him seated between them, his head came to rest on one of his shoulders. Sally thought he was staring at her. She buried her head in a book and tried not to notice.

At Twenty-eighth Street, one of the men stood up.

"Take it easy, Jim," he said to the man in the middle, and he got off.

At Twenty-third Street, Jim's other friend stood up.

"You'll be fine," he said, and he got off.

Now the only ones left in the car were Jim and Sally. Just then the train went around a sharp curve, and Jim pitched onto the floor at Sally's feet. When she looked down at him, she saw a trickle of blood on the side of his head and, just above it, a bullet hole.

· *THE CAT IN A SHOPPING BAG* ·

Mrs. Briggs was driving to the shopping mall to do some last-minute Christmas shopping when she accidentally ran over a cat. She could not bear to leave the corpse on the road for other cars to hit and squash. So she stopped, wrapped the cat in some tissue paper she had with her, and put it in an old shopping bag in the backseat. She would bury it in the backyard when she got home.

At the mall, she parked her car and began walking to one of the stores. She had taken only a few steps when, out of the corner of her eye, she saw a woman reach into the open window of her car and take the shopping bag with the dead cat. Then the woman quickly got into a car nearby and drove away.

Mrs. Briggs ran back to her car and followed the woman. She caught up with her at a diner down the road. She followed her inside and watched the woman slide into a booth and give a waitress her order.

As the woman sat sipping her soda, she reached into Mrs. Briggs' shopping bag. Then she bent down and looked inside. A look of horror crossed her face. She screamed, and fainted.

The waitress called an ambulance. Two attendants carried the woman away on a stretcher. But they left the shopping bag behind. Mrs. Briggs picked up the bag and ran after them.

"This is hers," she called. "It's her Christmas present! She wouldn't want to lose it."

· *THE BED BY THE WINDOW* ·

The three old men shared a room at the nursing home.
Their room had only one window, but for them it was the only link to the real world. Ted Conklin, who had

been there the longest, had the bed next to the window. When Ted died, the man in the next bed, George Best, took his place; and the third man, Richard Greene, took George's bed.

Despite his illness, George was a cheerful man who spent his days describing the sights he could see from his bed—pretty girls, a policeman on horseback, a traffic jam, a pizza parlor, a fire station and other scenes of life outside.

Richard loved to listen to George. But the more George talked about life outside, the more Richard wanted to *see* it for himself. Yet he knew that only when George died would he have his chance. He wanted to look out that window so badly that one day he decided to kill George. "He is going to die soon, anyway," he told himself. "What difference would it make?"

George had a bad heart. If he had an attack during the night and a nurse could not get to him right away, he had pills he could take. He kept them in a bottle on top of the cabinet between his bed and Richard's. All Richard had to do was knock the bottle to the floor where George could not reach it.

A few nights later George died just as Richard had planned he would. And the next morning Richard was moved to the bed by the window. Now he would see for himself all the things outside that George had described.

After the nurses had left, Richard turned to the window and looked out. But all he could see was a blank brick wall.

· THE DEAD MAN'S HAND ·

The students at the school for nurses got along quite well with one another, except for Alice. The trouble with Alice was that she was perfect. At least that is how it seemed to the other students.

She was always friendly and always cheerful. Nothing ever upset her. Her school assignments were always on time, and always perfect. She didn't even bite her fingernails.

Many of the student nurses resented Alice. They would have liked to see her fail at something—become frightened, or cry, or do something that showed she had weaknesses like they did.

One night several students tried to frighten Alice with a practical joke. They borrowed the hand of a corpse they had been studying in anatomy and tied it to the light cord in her closet. When she tried to turn on the light, she would find herself holding a dead man's hand. "That would scare anybody," one of them said. "If it doesn't scare her, nothing will."

After tying the hand in place, they went to the movies. When they got back, Alice was asleep. But when they didn't see her the next morning, they decided to find out what had happened.

There was no sign of Alice in her room. But they soon found her. She was sitting on the floor in her closet

staring at the dead man's hand and mumbling to herself. Alice didn't even look up.

The "joke" had worked, but nobody was laughing.

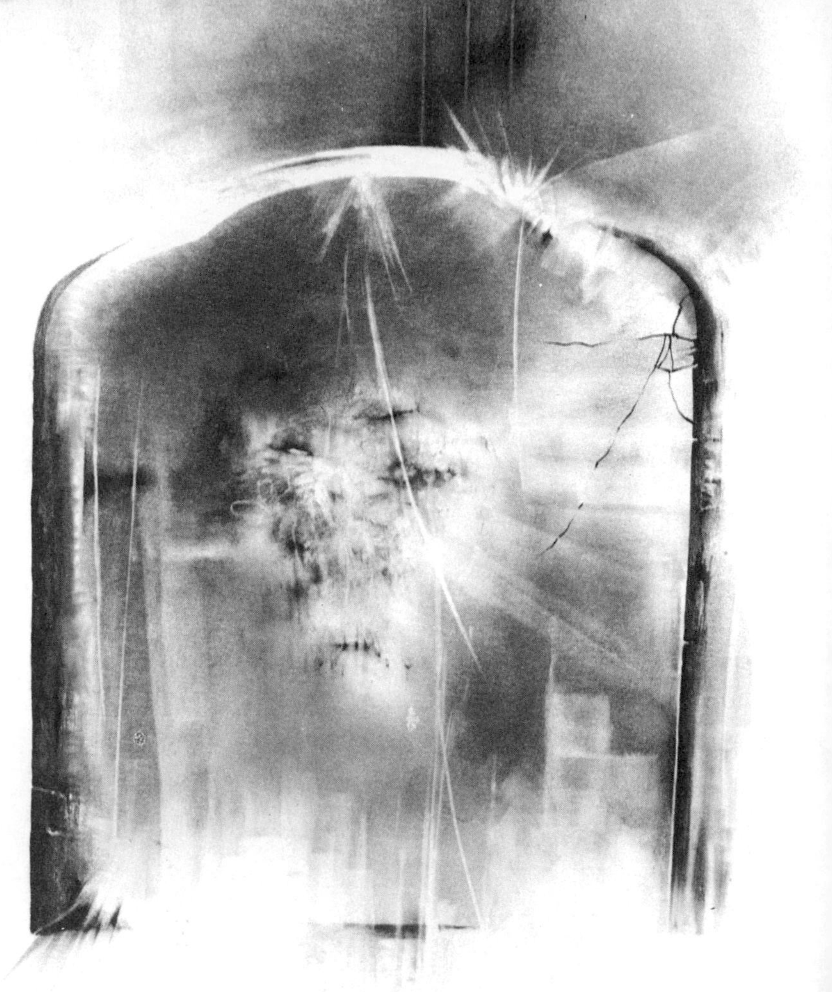

· *A GHOST IN THE MIRROR* ·

This is a scary game that young people sometimes play—trying to conjure up a ghost in their bathroom mirror. Many don't *really* believe that a ghost is going to appear. But they try to raise one anyway, for the fun and the excitement.

Some are willing to settle for any ghost, but others have a particular ghost in mind. One of these is a ghost named Mary Worth, who also is known as Mary Jane and Bloody Mary. She is the heroine of an old comic strip, but some say she actually was a witch who was hanged at the infamous witch trials in Salem, Massachusetts, in 1692.

Another of these ghosts is "*La Llorona*," the weeping woman who wanders the streets of cities and towns from Texas to California and throughout Mexico, looking for her lost child.

Still another is Mary Whales, a young woman who is supposed to have been killed in a car accident in Indianapolis, Indiana, about 1965. Her ghost is one of the "vanishing hitchhikers." It is said that again and again she thumbs a ride home in a passing car, then vanishes before she gets there.

Here is how ghost hunters try to raise a ghost:

1. They find a quiet bathroom, close the door, and turn off the lights.
2. While they stare at their face in the mirror, they repeat the ghost's name, usually forty-seven times or a hundred times. If any ghost will do, they say "any ghost" in place of a name. If they do manage to raise one, its face will slowly replace their face in the mirror.

Some say a ghost is likely to be angry at being disturbed. If it gets angry enough, they say, it will try to shatter the mirror and come right into the room. But a player can always turn on the lights and send the ghost back to where it came from. And when that happens, the game is over.

· THE CURSE ·

My dad's friend, Charlie Potter, was a small, nervous man who was always looking around, as if he was in some kind of danger. After he told me this story about his college fraternity, I understood why.

"The frat doesn't exist anymore," he said. "It was banned years ago. We had just nine members at that point and were taking in two more: Jack Lawton and Ernie Kramer.

"One night in January, just about this time of year, the nine of us took them out into the country for their initiation. We took them to an old deserted house where two young men about our age had been murdered recently. Their murderer was still at large.

"We gave Jack a lighted candle and told him to go up to the third floor. 'Stay there for an hour,' we told him, 'then come back down. Don't speak. Don't make any noise. If your candle goes out, carry on in the dark.'

"From where we were standing, we could see the light from Jack's candle moving up the stairs to the second floor, then to the third. But when he got to the third floor, his candle went out.

"We guessed that he had come to a drafty corner, and the wind blew it out. But when the hour went by and he didn't come down, we weren't so sure. We waited another fifteen minutes and got more and more nervous.

"So we sent Ernie Kramer up after him. When Ernie got to the third floor, his candle also went out. We waited ten minutes, twenty minutes, but there was no sign of either of them. 'Come on down,' we called, but they didn't answer.

"Finally, we decided to go and get them. Armed with flashlights, we started up the stairs. It was as quiet and dark as a grave in that house. When we got to the second floor, we called out again, but there was no answer.

"When we got to the third floor, we walked into a great big open space like an attic. Jack and Ernie weren't there. But we saw footprints in the dust. These led to a room on the other side of the attic.

"That room was also empty. But there was fresh blood on the floor, and the window was wide open. It was about twenty-five feet to the ground, but there was no ladder or rope in sight that they could have used to get down.

"We searched the rest of the house and the land around the house and found nothing. We decided that they were playing a trick on us. We figured that in some way they had escaped through the window and were hiding in the woods. The blood on the floor was to throw us off the track. We guessed that they'd show up the next day with a lot of stories and a lot of laughs. But they didn't.

"The next day we told the Dean of Men what had happened, and he reported it to the police. The police didn't find anything either, and after several weeks the search ended. To this day no one knows what happened to Jack Lawton and Ernie Kramer.

"There isn't much more to tell," he said. "We weren't arrested, but the college disbanded the fraternity and suspended the nine of us from school for a year.

"The strangest part came after we graduated. Someone must have placed a curse on us. Every year since then, around the time of that initiation, one of us has died or gone crazy.

"I'm the only one left," he said, "and I'm in pretty good health. But there are times when I feel just a little peculiar. . . ."

(Now rush at someone in the audience and SCREAM:)

AAAAAAAAAAH!

The Last Laugh

These stories are scary and *funny.*

· THE CHURCH ·

There was a fellow named Larry Berger who wasn't afraid of anybody alive. But anybody who was dead scared the wits out of him.

One night Larry was out driving in the country in his old jeep when he got caught in a bad thunderstorm. The rain was coming down in sheets. Since his jeep didn't have a top to it, Larry started looking for a place to take shelter.

But at the first place he came to he didn't even slow down. It was an old deserted cabin, probably as dry as a bone inside. But Larry knew for a fact that it was haunted, and he wasn't going to stay there.

A few miles farther, he came to an old abandoned church standing all alone in a field. It hadn't been used in years. All the window glass was gone, but it still had sections of the roof intact. So Larry parked his jeep and ran inside.

It was as dark as could be in there. Larry groped around until he found a pew and sat down. It was nice and dry, just as he had thought it would be, and he stretched out his legs and made himself comfortable.

Suddenly there was a big flash of lightning, and Larry saw that he wasn't the only one in that church. There were people sitting in almost every pew. They all had their heads bowed as if they were praying, and they all were dressed in white.

"These must be ghosts sitting in their shrouds," Larry thought. "They must have come in from some graveyard to get dry."

Larry jumped up and ran down the aisle as fast as he could, right smack into one of the ghosts. And the ghost, he went—BAA-A-A!

· *THE BAD NEWS* ·

Leon and Todd loved baseball. When they were young, they had played on the town's baseball team. Leon had been the pitcher, and Todd had played second base. Now that they were a lot older, they spent their free time watching baseball games on TV and talking about baseball.

"Do you think they play baseball in Heaven?" Leon asked Todd one day.

"That's a good question," said Todd. "The one who gets there first should let the other one know somehow."

As it turned out, Todd got to Heaven first, and Leon waited patiently to hear from him. One day Leon found Todd sitting in the living room waiting for him.

Leon was very excited to see him. "What is it like up there?" he asked. "And what about baseball?"

"When it comes to baseball," said Todd, "I have some good news, and I have some bad news. The good news is that we do play baseball in Heaven. We have some fine teams. I play second base on my team, just like I used to in the old days. That's the good news."

"What's the bad news?" asked Leon.

"The bad news," said Todd, "is that you are scheduled to pitch tomorrow."

· CEMETERY SOUP ·

On her way home from the market, the woman took a short cut through the cemetery. There, sticking up out of the ground, she saw a big bone. She picked it up and looked it over carefully.

"This will make a very good soup bone," she said. "I think I'll take it home. It's perfect weather for hot soup."

When she got home, the first thing she did was start the soup. Into the big soup pot went water, carrots, green beans, corn, barley, onions, potatoes, a snitch of beef, some salt and pepper, and—the bone. She brought it all to a boil, then brought it down to a simmer.

"Yum!" she said, sniffing it and tasting it. "I can hardly wait till supper."

Suddenly she heard a small voice.

"Please give me back my bone."

The woman paid no attention. Soon she heard the voice again.

"May I have back my bone, please?"

The woman was reading the newspaper, and again she didn't take any notice. In a little while, the voice spoke up once more. It was beginning to sound angry.

"Give me back my bone!"

The woman kept on reading the paper.

"Some people are too impatient," she muttered.

Once more the voice spoke. Now it sounded *very* angry, and it was so loud that the whole house shook.

"I WANT MY BONE BACK!"

The woman reached into the pot, grabbed the bone, and threw it out the window. In a voice just as loud, she shouted,

"TAKE IT!"

There was an eerie silence. Then the woman heard footsteps scurrying away from the house down the road toward the cemetery. And she got up and served herself some soup.

· *THE BROWN SUIT* ·

A woman came to the funeral parlor to see her husband's corpse.

"You did a good job," she said to the undertaker. "He looks just the way he always looked, except for one thing. My husband always wore a brown suit, but you have him dressed in a blue suit."

"That is no problem," said the undertaker. "We can easily change it."

When she returned later, her husband was wearing a brown suit.

"Now he looks just the way he always did," she said. "I know you went to a lot of trouble."

"It was no trouble," he said. "As it happened, there is a man here who was wearing a brown suit, and his widow felt that blue would be better. He is about your husband's size. So we gave him the blue one and gave your husband the brown one."

"Even so," she said, "changing all that clothing was a big job."

"Not really," said the undertaker. "All we did was exchange their heads."

· *BA-ROOOM!* ·

O'Leary is dead,
and O'Riley don't know it.
O'Riley is dead,
and O'Leary don't know it.
They both are dead
in the very same bed,
and neither one knows
that the other one's dead.
BA-ROOOM! BA-ROOOM!

To the tune of "The Irish Washerwoman"

O' - Lea - ry is dead and O' - Ri - ley don't know it, O' -
Ri - ley is dead and O' - Lea - ry don't know it, They
both_ are dead in the ver - y same bed And_
nei - ther one knows that the oth - er one's dead. BA-ROOOM!_ BA-ROOOM!

· *THUMPITY-THUMP* ·

When we moved to Schenectady from Schoharie, we rented a house awful cheap 'cause it was spooked, and nobody would live in it. But we didn't care, 'cause we didn't take no stock in spooks.

We had just gone to bed the first night, dog tired from riding in a wagon all day. We hadn't had time to shut our eyes when we heard a *thumpity-thump, thumpity-thump* comin' down the attic stairs. I covered my head with the blankets, but I couldn't shut out the sound. *Thumpity-thump, thumpity-thump,* it went. I could hear it plain as day.

Past the bedroom door *thumpity-thump, thumpity-thump* and down the stairs *thumpity-thump, thumpity-thump* and through the kitchen *thumpity-thump, thumpity-thump* and down the cellar stairs *thumpity-thump, thumpity-thump,* makin' the most awful racket you ever heard. It was more than we could stand. So we all followed the sound to see what was goin' on.

When we got down the cellar stairs, we saw that it was a chair that had made all of that racket. There it was, with one of its legs pointin' to a place on the dirt floor. We all just stood and gawped till my brother Ike said that he believed that the chair was trying to tell us something about the place it was pointing at.

So Ike went and got a shovel and started diggin'. He

didn't have to dig far before his shovel struck somethin' hard. Pretty soon we could see the edge of a box stickin' out. We all hollered for him to hurry up and uncover the rest of it. And the chair—it got so excited, it jumped up and down like it had gone plumb crazy.

When Ike got the box uncovered, Pop and the boys pried off the lid. And there was the body of a man all smooched with blood. It was plain as the nose on your face that he had been murdered, and the chair wanted folks to know it. Right then and there we decided to leave. Bein' strangers, everybody would think that we had murdered him and come there to hide the body. It didn't take us long to fill up that hole and get out of that house.

The chair was awful mad about our leavin', and it went up the cellar stairs ***thumpity-thump, thumpity-thump*** louder than when it had gone down. Then it ***thumpity-thump***ed up the next set of stairs and the next louder still. When it got back into the attic, it ***THUMPITY-THUMP***ED so loud we thought it would thump all the plasterin' down on our heads.

Nobody asked us why we were movin' out so soon, 'cause nobody ever stayed more than one night in that place, and most not that long. But I can tell you we were thankful to get back to Schoharie where chairs stay where they're put and don't go rarin' and rampagin' 'roun, scarin' folks out of their wits, pointin' out murders and goodness knows what!

ABBREVIATIONS IN NOTES, SOURCES, AND BIBLIOGRAPHY

AF	*Arkansas Folklore*
CFQ	*California Folklore Quarterly*
HF	*Hoosier Folklore*
HFB	*Hoosier Folklore Bulletin*
IF	*Indiana Folklore*
IUFA	Indiana University Folklore Archive, Bloomington, Ind.
JAF	*Journal of American Folklore*
KFQ	*Kentucky Folklore Quarterly*
NEFA	Northeast Archives of Folklore and Oral History, University of Maine, Orono, Me.
PTFS	Publication of the Texas Folklore Society
SFQ	*Southern Folklore Quarterly*
SS	Alvin Schwartz, *Scary Stories to Tell in the Dark*
WF	*Western Folklore*

Notes

The publications cited are described in the Bibliography.

Hoo-Ha's (Introduction): The term "heebie-jeebies" comes from a pre-World War I comic-strip cartoonist named W. DeBeck. The term "screaming meemies" was the name first given to the whistling shells that the German army fired at the Allies during World War I. Various dictionaries.

Living Ghosts (Chapter 1): There has always been a belief that the dead can return to our world in ghost form, if they have a need to do so. They may be invisible, or rise up like a drifting mist, or appear as they did when they were alive. Of these living ghosts, the best known are the ghostly or vanishing hitchhikers. There are many tales about them. Usually there is a main character who dies, then makes repeated efforts to return home or to familiar surroundings. The ghost manages to hitchhike a ride in a passing car, but always vanishes just before the car reaches its destination. There are several tales of living ghosts in Chapter 1: "Something Was Wrong," "The Wreck," and "One Sunday Morning." For a detailed discussion of ghosts, see *SS*, pp. 92–94.

"One Sunday Morning" (p. 6): This tale is rooted in the ancient belief that the night belongs to the dead and that places of worship are haunted after dark.

The scholar Alexander Krappe suggested that it may also be rooted in a dream, possibly in an experience in which the dreamer walked in her sleep. It might be, he said, that the dreamer actually walked to the site of the dream and continued dreaming until she awakened, and in that way provided a basis for a tale. What if she found on awakening, as

Ida did, that her clothes had been torn or that she had suffered a bad scratch? Such things could be explained in a number of ways, he said.

Krappe told of a German physician in the nineteenth century. When he was in high school, the physician lived in the same house with a seventeen-year-old boy who walked in his sleep. One night the boy dreamed that it was seven o'clock in the morning and time to go to school.

While still asleep, he washed, dressed, got his books together, and went downstairs. On his way out the door, he stopped to check the time, as he did every morning. Just then the clock struck midnight, chiming twelve times, and awakened him.

Had the boy not awakened, Krappe suggested that he probably would have gone to school, just as Ida in "One Sunday Morning" went to church where she continued to dream. See Krappe, *Balor*, pp. 114–25; *JAF* 60: pp. 159–62.

"Sounds" (p. 8): The person who found this legend was a newspaperman from Brooklyn, N.Y., named Charles M. Skinner. Although not a trained folklorist, Skinner was the first serious collector of American legends. Between 1896 and 1903 he compiled five books of legends from throughout the United States and its possessions, some of which became best-sellers. In all, Skinner found and retold 515 legends dealing with ghosts, treasures, Indian uprisings, witches, rescues, and other subjects. Only in recent years have folklorists become interested in such material. See Dorson, "Skinner."

"Somebody Fell from Aloft" (p. 12): A writer and artist named George S. Wasson was the author of this tale and others that suggested the kinds of stories being told in Maine fishing villages during the nineteenth century. They were based on his knowledge of the local tales and dialects in such places. All involved a small port named Killick Cove, actually

Kittery Point in southern Maine, where Wasson lived. See Dorson, *Jonathan*, pp. 243–48.

"Clinkity-Clink" (p. 20): This is one of the famous Uncle Remus stories that Joel Chandler Harris created from Negro tales, songs, customs, and ways of speaking he learned as a white boy in the Old South.

His stories on Negro plantation life first appeared in 1878 in the newspaper *The Atlanta Constitution*. The first of his books, *Uncle Remus: His Songs and Sayings*, appeared two years later and brought him fame. Nine other collections followed, including *Uncle Remus and Brer Rabbit* and *The Tar Baby and Other Rhymes of Uncle Remus*.

They evoked a remarkable sense of the life and character of the Negro in the Old South, with Uncle Remus serving the traditional role of an elderly Negro, storyteller to the master's children. See Brookes, pp. 3–21; 43–62.

Buried Alive (p. 29, "Rings on Her Fingers"): When a dead person is embalmed, a fluid commonly containing formaldehyde is pumped into the blood and lymph systems. It preserves the body for a long time. It also assures that the person who is being buried is dead.

Before modern methods of embalming became widespread, there were many legends like "Rings on Her Fingers." Each told of how some person had been given up for dead when actually they were in a coma or trance of some kind, and regained consciousness during their funeral or after they had been buried. In the latter case, those who were rescued from a horrible death owed their lives to grave robbers.

In those years thieves dug up corpses for their jewels, or they stole the corpses and sold them to medical schools. Now and then they found a living person who was revived by the shock of cold air or by the efforts they were making to cut off one of their fingers. See Sources for "Rings."

In the early 1800s an English woman was so concerned

about being buried alive, she arranged to be buried in a funeral vault in a coffin without a lid. A small opening was left in the wall of the vault so that she could breathe and be heard if she regained consciousness. See Hole, p. 54.

Vampires (p. 37): The vampire in the tale "The Window" is a living corpse, a person who died but is not always dead. It cannot rest in its grave. It spends each night searching for a human from whose throat it can suck the blood it needs. But by cockcrow it must return to its coffin.

People in many parts of the world believe in vampires. But the belief is strongest and most widespread in Russia, Poland, Rumania, Bulgaria, Hungary, and Greece. In eighteenth-century Hungary, the outcry over the threat of vampires was as great as the concern over witches in New England a hundred years earlier.

There are few detailed accounts of vampire experiences in America or the British Isles. One is a brief tale collected in 1933 in Crane, Missouri, by Vance Randolph. It tells of a boy who went into a witch's yard to retrieve a ball he had been playing with. The witch's daughter cut his throat and, with her mother, drank his blood. Randolph suggests that it is related to the ballad "Sir Hugh," which involves a similar incident.

The English story "The Window" is probably one of the most detailed of the English-language accounts. However, the description of the method used to destroy the vampire may not have been complete. In the Eastern European tradition, the vampire would have been decapitated before it was cremated. Then its remains would have been buried at a crossroads. There also is one other traditional method of ensuring the vampire will not return: driving a sharpened wooden stake through the vampire's heart.

It is said that only certain people become vampires: witches, suicides, and persons who were bitten by a vampire. If a corpse is buried with its mouth open or a cat jumps over the corpse while it is being buried, the corpse will also become a vampire.

It is said that the best way to ward off a vampire is to wear bells, garlic, or iron in some form.

See Leach, *Dictionary*, p. 1154; Randolph, *Church House*, pp. 164–65; *Ozark Folksongs*, vol. 1, pp. 148–51; Belden, pp. 69–73.

Horror Stories (p. 49, "Oh, Susannah!"): This is one of a group of unusually popular legends about atrocities committed by mad killers at loose on or near college campuses. They include stories of young people who have been struck with an ax or stabbed with a knife, whose cries for help are ignored because their roommates are too frightened to open the door to their room. The folklorist Linda Dégh suggests that these legends are modern cautionary tales warning young people of the dangers that threaten them as they are increasingly on their own. See Barnes, 307–12; Dégh, "The Roommate's Death," *IF* 2; *SS*, 96–97.

Poltergeists (p. 79, "Thumpity-Thump"): The haunted chair in this story is a poltergeist, a term that means literally "noise ghost." However, such a ghost usually is invisible. It makes its presence known through knocking and rapping sounds and other noises and actions for which there is no explanation.

Such ghosts are said to move furniture, cause dishes to fly from cupboards and crash to the floor, hurl burning chunks of wood from fireplaces, and even cut clothing and blankets into strange shapes, often crescents, with invisible shears. See Gardner, pp. 96–97; Musick, *West Virginia*, p. 42; Lawson and Porter, 371–82.

In *Pickwick Papers*, Dickens tells of a talking chair that helps a traveling salesman win the hand of the woman he wants to marry. See Dickens, pp. 188–96.

Sources

The sources of each item are given, along with variants and related information. When available, names of collectors (C) and informants (I) are given. The publications cited are described in the Bibliography.

INTRODUCTION

p. xi *Hoo-Ha's:* From a T. S. Eliot poem, "Fragment of an Agon." See Eliot, p. 84.

WHEN SHE SAW HIM, SHE SCREAMED AND RAN

p. 3 *"Something Was Wrong"*: Retelling of an untitled story in Cerf, *Try and Stop Me*, pp. 275–76.

p. 4 *"The Wreck"*: Based on a brief reference in Parochetti, 55. This is one of the many "ghostly hitchhiker" stories in which a young woman is given a ride home in a car, then turns out to be a ghost. See Beardsley, Richard K., *CFQ* 1: 303–36; *CFQ* 2: 3–25; *SS*: p. 121. See the Note "Living Ghosts."

p. 6 *"One Sunday Morning"*: I first heard this tale as a student at Northwestern University, Evanston, Ill., in the 1950s. The text is based on my recollections, but also on references in Krappe, *Balor*, pp. 114–25, and Krappe, *JAF* 60: 159–62. See the Note "One Sunday Morning."

p. 8 *"Sounds"*: Based on a legend in Mobile, Alabama, toward the end of the nineteenth century. The deserted house described in the text was built by a wealthy Englishman who lived there with his daughter, who he said was "half-witted," and several servants. No one visited them, and they seldom went out. He abruptly returned to England without her. She disappeared. The house was sold again and again. No one could live there. See Skinner, pp. 17–19. See the Note "Sounds."

p. 11 *"A Weird Blue Light"*: Retold from a newspaper report in the Downey, Cal., *Champion*, Dec. 17, 1892, taken from the Galveston, Tex., *True Flag*, n.d., reprinted in Splitter, p. 209.

p. 12 *"Somebody Fell from Aloft"*: Adapted and abridged from a story in Wasson, "Who Fell from Aloft?", pp. 106–28. See the Note "Somebody Fell from Aloft."

p. 17 *"The Little Black Dog"*: This tale of a dog seeking revenge is adapted from the Ozark Mountains story "Si Burton's Little Black Dog," (I): Mrs. Marie Wilbur, Pineville, Mo., 1929. See Randolph, *Church House*, pp. 171–73.

p. 20 *"Clinkity-Clink"*: A late-nineteenth-century Southern Negro version of the well-known jump story "The Golden Arm," in which a golden arm or some other part of the body is stolen from a corpse who returns from the grave to claim it. It is adapted from Harris, "A Ghost Story," *Nights with Uncle Remus*, pp. 164–69. See the Note "Clinkity-Clink."

SHE WAS SPITTIN' AND YOWLIN' JUST LIKE A CAT

p. 27 *"The Bride"*: Retelling of a traditional English and American tale, based on variants and the lyrics of the ballad "The Mistletoe Bough" by the songwriter Thomas Haynes Bayly. This is the last verse:

At length an oak chest that had long lain hid,
Was found in the castle; they raised the lid,
And a skeleton form lay mouldering there
In the bridal wreath of the lady fair.
Oh, sad was her fate; in sporting jest
She hid from her lord in the old oak chest;
It closed with a spring, and her bridal bloom
Lay withering there in a living tomb.

There was even a play about the unfortunate bride, "The Mistletoe Bough; or the Fatal Chest" by Charles A. Somerset. See Briggs and Tongue, pp. 88; Disher, pp. 89–90.

p. 29 *"Rings on Her Fingers"*: Retold from several variants. Dorson, *Buying the Wind*, pp. 310–11; Baylor, "Folklore from Socorro, New Mexico," pp. 100–102. The conclusion in which the grave robber dies was suggested by the fate of "The Thievish Sexton," Briggs and Tongue, pp. 88–89. See the Note "Buried Alive."

p. 31 *"The Drum"*: Cautionary tales warning children to behave or suffer the consequences are found in most cultures. "The Drum" is a retelling of such a story which was passed down by several generations of an English family, then migrated to America with another family member. In the retelling in this book, the title has been shortened from "The Pear Drum," and the names of the children have been changed from "Blue-Eyes" and "Turkey" to "Dolores" and "Sandra." See the text and letter from J. Y. Bell and the letter from Lilian H. Hayward, in which she recalls a literary version of such a story that appeared in England during the late nineteenth century, *Folklore 66* (1955): 302–4, 431.

The folklorist Katharine M. Briggs regards the gypsy girl in the story as a kind of Satan in offering the drum in return for evil behavior, but as more evil; for the girl goes back on her bargain, something Satan would not do. Briggs, Part A, Vol. 2, pp. 554–55.

p. 37 *"The Window"*: Adapted and abridged from Hare, pp. 50–52. See the Note "Vampires."

p. 40 *"Wonderful Sausage"*: Retold from several variants and a song. See Randolph, "The Bloody Miller," *Turtle*, pp. 138–40, (I): Mrs. Elizabeth Maddocks, Joplin, Mo., 1937; Edwards, p. 8, an Arkansas variant; and Saxon, p. 258, a New Orleans legend in which a sausage maker grinds his wife into sausage and is driven mad by her ghost.

The song is entitled "Donderback's Machine," or just "Donderback," with various spellings, and minor variations. It concludes when Donderback's sausage grinder breaks down, and he climbs inside to repair it:

His wife she had the nightmare,
She walked right in her sleep,
She grabbed the crank, gave it a yank,
and Donderback was meat.

It is sung to the tune of "The Son of a Gambolier," which became the tune for "I'm a Ramblin' Wreck from Georgia Tech." See Spaeth, p. 90; Randolph, *Ozark Folksongs*, vol. 3, pp. 488–89.

p. 42 *"The Cat's Paw"*: Retold from a widespread witch tale. See Randolph, *Ozark Mountain Folks*, p. 37; Randolph, "The Cat's Foot," *Turtle*, pp. 174–75, (I): Lon Jordon, Farmington, Ark., 1941; Puckett, p. 149; Gardner, p. 174; Porter, p. 115.

p. 45 *"The Voice"*: Traditional jump story, to which the compiler added the two concluding lines. See *SS*, p. 7, p. 14; Opie, p. 36; Saxon, p. 277.

WHEN I WAKE UP, EVERYTHING WILL BE ALL RIGHT

p. 49 *"Oh, Susannah!"*: A well-known legend among college students, this frequently is entitled "The Roommate's Death." The text in this book is retold from a number of variants: NEFA, (I): Linda Mansfield, (C): Mary Dudley, Orono, Me., 1964; IUFA, (I): Shelly Herbst, (C): Diane Pavy, Bloomington, Ind., 1960; questionnaire interview by the compiler with Lin Rogove, Lancaster, Pa., 1982; *IF* 3 (1970): 67. See the Note "Horror Stories."

p. 50 *"The Man in the Middle"*: This legend has been told in New York, London, Paris, and other big cities with subways. Around the turn of the century the same story was being told about a horse car, a horse-drawn bus in New York as it moved south on Fifth Avenue in a snowstorm. See "Folklore in the News": *WF* 8: 174; Clough, pp. 355–56.

p. 52 *"The Cat in a Shopping Bag"*: I first heard this story in the late 1970s in Denver and Helena, Montana. Text is based on my recollections and similar versions in Brunvand, pp. 108–9, collected in the Salt Lake City area in 1975.

p. 54 *"The Bed by the Window"*: Retold from Cerf, *Try and Stop Me*, pp. 288–89.

p. 56 *"The Dead Man's Hand"*: A tale told in medical and nursing schools. Retold from variants in Parochetti, p. 53, and Baughman, "The Cadaver Arm," pp. 30–32. In another variant, the victim is found dead with the dead man's hand clutching his throat, Barnes, p. 307.

p. 58 *"A Ghost in the Mirror"*: Based on references in Knapp,

p. 242; Langlois, pp. 196–204; Perez, pp. 73–74, 76.

p. 60 *"The Curse"*: A retelling of a legend frequently entitled "The Fatal Fraternity Initiation." It is based on several variants: Baughman, "The Fatal Initiation," *HFB* 4: 49–55; NEFA, (I): Linette Bridges, (C): Patricia J. Curtis, Blue Hill, Me., 1967; Dégh, *Indiana Folklore: A Reader*, pp. 159–60.

THE LAST LAUGH

p. 67 *"The Church"*: Retold from a text in Randolph, *Sticks*, pp. 24–25, (I): Wayne Hogue, Memphis, Tenn., 1952.

p. 69 *"The Bad News"*: (I): Constance Paras, 12, Winchester-Thurston School, Pittsburgh, 1983.

p. 71 *"Cemetery Soup"*: This jump story is based on a tale in Puckett, pp. 124–25, (I): Marie Sneed, Burton, S.C., about 1925. For a similar English version, see Gilchrist, pp. 378–79.

p. 75 *"The Brown Suit"*: Compiler's recollection.

p. 76 *"BA-ROOOM!"*: Lyrics, (I): Margaret Z. Fisher, Manheim Township, Pa., 1982. Music, "The Irish Washerwoman," a traditional dance tune played in fast jig time. Musical notation transcribed by Barbara C. Schwartz, Princeton, N.J., 1984, from a performance on the dulcimer by Thomas Mann, Ortonville, Iowa, 1937, tape recorded by Mrs. Sidney R. Cowell, in the recording "Folk Music of the United States, Play and Dance Songs and Tunes," ed., B. A. Botkin, Library of Congress Music Division, AAFSL9.

p. 79 *"Thumpity-Thump"*: Adapted from Gardner, pp. 96–97, (I): Maggie Zee, Middleburgh, N.Y., about 1914. See the Note "Poltergeists."

Bibliography

BOOKS

Books that may be of interest to young people are marked with an asterisk (*).

Baker, Ronald L. *Hoosier Folk Legends.* Bloomington, Ind.: Indiana University Press, 1982.

Belden, Henry M. *Ballads and Songs Collected by the Missouri Folklore Society,* vol. 15. Columbia, Mo.: University of Missouri, 1940.

Bennett, John. *The Doctor to the Dead: Grotesque Legends & Folk Tales of Old Charleston.* New York: Rinehart & Co., 1943.

Botkin, Benjamin A., ed. *A Treasury of American Folklore.* New York: Crown Publishers, 1944.

———, ed. *A Treasury of New England Folklore.* New York: Crown Publishers, Inc., 1965.

Briggs, Katharine M. *A Dictionary of British Folktales.* 4 vols. Bloomington, Ind.: Indiana University Press, 1967.

Briggs, Katharine M., and Ruth L. Tongue. *Folktales of England.* Chicago, Ill.: University of Chicago Press, 1965.

Brookes, Stella B. *Joel Chandler Harris—Folklorist,* Athens, Ga.: University of Georgia Press, 1950.

Brunvand, Jan H. *The Vanishing Hitchhiker: American Urban Legends and Their Meanings.* New York: W. W. Norton & Co., 1981.

*Cerf, Bennett A. *Famous Ghost Stories.* New York: Random House, 1944.

———. *Try and Stop Me.* New York: Simon and Schuster,

1944. Reprint Edition: Garden City, N.Y.: Garden City Books, 1954.
Clough, Ben C., ed. *The American Imagination at Work: Tall Tales and Folk Tales.* New York: Alfred A. Knopf, 1947.
Dégh, Linda. "The 'Belief Legend' in Modern Society: Form, Function and Relationship to Other Genres." In Wayland D. Hand, ed. *American Folk Legend, A Symposium.* Berkeley, Cal.: University of California Press, 1971.
———, ed. *Indiana Folklore: A Reader.* Bloomington, Ind.: University of Indiana Press, 1980.
Dickens, Charles. *Pickwick Papers: The Posthumous Papers of the Pickwick Club.* New York: The Heritage Press, 1938.
Disher, Maurice W. *Victorian Song: From Dive to Drawing Room.* London: Phoenix House, 1955.
Dorson, Richard M. *American Folklore.* Chicago, Ill.: University of Chicago Press, 1959.
———. "How Shall We Rewrite Charles M. Skinner Today?" In Wayland D. Hand, ed. *American Folk Legend, A Symposium.* Berkeley, Cal.: University of California Press, 1971.
———. *Jonathan Draws the Long Bow.* Cambridge, Mass.: Harvard University Press, 1946.
———, ed. *Bloodstoppers and Bearwalkers.* Cambridge, Mass.: Harvard University Press, 1952.
———, ed. *Buying the Wind.* Chicago: University of Chicago Press, 1964.
———, ed. *Negro Tales from Calvin, Michigan.* Bloomington, Ind.: Indiana University Press, 1958.
Eliot, T. S. *The Complete Poems and Plays, 1909–1950.* New York: Harcourt, Brace & World, 1952.
Gardner, Emelyn E. *Folklore from the Schoharie Hills, New York.* Ann Arbor, Mich.: University of Michigan Press, 1937.
Hare, Augustus, J. C. *The Story of My Life.* London: George Allen & Unwin, Ltd., 1950. An abridgement of Vols. 4, 5, and 6 of *The Story of My Life,* George Allen, 1900.

Harris, Joel Chandler. *Nights with Uncle Remus: Myths and Legends of the Old Plantation.* Boston: James R. Osgood & Co., 1882.

______. Richard Chase, ed. *The Complete Tales of Uncle Remus.* Boston: Houghton Mifflin Company, 1955.

Hole, Christina. *Haunted England: A Survey of English Ghost-Lore.* London: B. T. Batsford, 1950.

Janvier, Thomas A. *Legends of the City of Mexico.* New York: Harper & Brothers, 1910.

*Jones, Louis C. *Things That Go Bump in the Night.* New York: Hill and Wang, 1959.

Knapp, Mary and Herbert. *One Potato, Two Potato: The Secret Education of American Children.* New York: W. W. Norton & Co., 1976.

Krappe, Alexander H. *Balor with the Evil Eye: Studies in Celtic and French Literature.* New York: *Institut des Études Françaises,* Columbia University, 1927.

Langlois, Janet. "Mary Whales, I Believe in You" in Linda Dégh, ed., *Indiana Folklore: A Reader.* See Dégh above.

*Leach, Maria. *Rainbow Book of American Folk Tales and Legends.* Cleveland and New York: World Publishing Co., 1959.

*______. *The Thing at the Foot of the Bed and Other Scary Stories.* Cleveland and New York: World Publishing Co., 1959.

*______. *Whistle in the Graveyard.* New York: The Viking Press, 1974.

______, ed. *Standard Dictionary of Folklore, Mythology and Legend.* New York: Funk & Wagnalls Publishing Co., 1972.

Musick, Ruth Ann. *Riddles, Folk Songs and Folk Tales from West Virginia.* Morgantown, W. Va.: West Virginia University Library, 1960.

Opie, Iona and Peter. *The Lore and Language of Schoolchildren.* London: Oxford University Press, 1959.

Puckett, Newbell N. *Folk Beliefs of the Southern Negro.* Chapel Hill, N. C.: University of North Carolina Press, 1926.

Randolph, Vance. *From an Ozark Holler: Stories of Ozark Mountain Folk.* New York: The Vanguard Press, 1933.
______. *Ozark Mountain Folks.* New York: The Vanguard Press, 1932.
______. *Ozark Superstitions.* New York: Columbia University Press, 1947. Reprint edition: *Ozark Magic and Folklore.* New York: Dover Publications, 1964.
______. "Witches, and Witch-Masters." In Benjamin A. Botkin, ed. *Folk-Say: A Regional Miscellany.* Norman, Okla.: University of Oklahoma Press, 1931.
______, ed. *Ozark Folksongs,* vols. 1, 3. Columbia, Mo.: State Society of Missouri, 1949.
______, ed. *Sticks in the Knapsack and Other Ozark Folk Tales.* New York: Columbia University Press, 1958.
______, ed. *The Talking Turtle and Other Ozark Folk Tales.* New York: Columbia University Press, 1957.
______, ed. *Who Blowed Up the Church House? And Other Ozark Folk Tales.* New York: Columbia University Press, 1952.
Saxon, Lyle *et al.* Louisiana Writers Project. *Gumbo Ya-Ya.* Boston: Houghton Mifflin Company, 1945.
*Schwartz, Alvin. *Scary Stories to Tell in the Dark.* New York: J. B. Lippincott, 1981.
Skinner, Charles M. *American Myths and Legends.* Vol. 2, Philadelphia: J. B. Lippincott Co., 1903.
Spaeth, Sigmund. *Read 'em and Weep, the Songs You Forgot to Remember.* Garden City, N.Y.: Doubleday, Page & Company, 1927.
Wasson, George S. *Captain Simeon's Store.* Boston: Houghton Mifflin Company, 1903.
Wilson, Charles M. "Folk Beliefs in the Ozark Hills." In Benjamin A. Botkin, ed. *Folk-Say: A Regional Miscellany.* Norman, Okla.: University of Oklahoma Press, 1930.

ARTICLES

Bacon, A. M., and Parsons, E. C. "Folk-Lore from Elizabeth City County, Va.": *JAF* 35 (1922): 250–327.

Barnes, Daniel R. "Some Functional Horror Stories on the Kansas University Campus." *SFQ* 30 (1966): 305–12.

Baughman, Ernest. "The Cadaver Arm." *HFB* 4 (1945): 30–32.

______. "The Fatal Initiation." *HFB* 4 (1945): 49–55.

Baylor, Dorothy J. "Buried Alive Stories, Folklore from Socorro, New Mexico, Part II." *HF* 6 (1947): 100–102.

Beardsley, Richard K., and Hankey, Rosalie. "The History of the Vanishing Hitchhiker." *CFQ* 2 (1943): 3–25.

______. "The Vanishing Hitchhiker": *CFQ* 1 (1942): 303–36.

Bell, J. Y. "The Pear Drum." *Folklore* 66 (1955): 302–4.

Boggs, Ralph Steele. "North Carolina White Folktales and Riddles." *JAF* 47 (1934): 3–25.

Dégh, Linda. "The Hook, the Boyfriend's Death, and the Killer in the Back Seat." *IF* 1 (1968): 98–106.

______. "The Roomate's Death and Related Dormitory Stories in Formation." *IF* 2 (1969): 55–74.

Dorson, Richard M. "The Folklore of Colleges." *The American Mercury* 68 (1949): 671–77.

______. "Polish Tales from Joe Woods." *WF* 8 (1949): 131–45.

Edwards, J. C. "Dunderbeck." *AF* 2 (1952): 8.

Fauset, Arthur Huff. "Tales and Riddles Collected in Philadelphia." *JAF* 41 (1928): 529–57.

"Folk Tales, Folklore in the News." *WF* 8 (1949): 174–75.

Gilchrist, A. G. "The Bone." *Folklore* 50 (1939): 378–79.

Grider, Sylvia. "Dormitory Legend-Telling in Process." *IF* 6 (1973): 1–32.

Hawes, Bess Lomax. "*La Llorona* in Juvenile Hall." *WF* 27: 153–70.
Hayward, Lilian H. "Correspondence." *Folklore* 66 (1955): 431.
Krappe, Alexander H. "The Spectres' Mass." *JAF* 60 (1947): 159–62.
Lawson, O. G., and Porter, Kenneth W. "Texas Poltergeist, 1881." *JAF* 64 (1951): 371–82.
Leddy, Betty. "*La Llorona* in Southern Arizona." *WF* 7 (1948): 272–77.
Parochetti, JoAnn S. "Scary Stories from Purdue." *KFQ* 10 (1965): 49–57.
Perez, Soledad. "Mexican Folklore from Austin, Texas." PTFS 24 (1951): 71–136.
Porter, F. Hampden. "Notes on the Folk-Lore of the Mountain Whites of the Alleghenies." *JAF* 7 (1894): 105–17.
Splitter, Henry W. "New Tales of American Phantom Ships." *WF* 9 (1950): 201–16.

ALVIN SCHWARTZ is known for a body of work of more than two dozen books of folklore for young readers that explore everything from wordplay and humor to tales and legends of all kinds. His collections of scary stories—SCARY STORIES TO TELL IN THE DARK, MORE SCARY STORIES TO TELL IN THE DARK, SCARY STORIES 3, and two I Can Read Books, IN A DARK, DARK ROOM and GHOSTS!—are just one part of his matchless folklore collection.

STEPHEN GAMMELL's drawings have appeared in a number of books for children, including SCARY STORIES TO TELL IN THE DARK, MORE SCARY STORIES TO TELL IN THE DARK, and SCARY STORIES 3. He is the winner of the Caldecott Medal for his drawings in SONG AND DANCE MAN by Karen Ackerman. His art in WHERE THE BUFFALOES BEGIN by Olaf Baker earned him a Caldecott Honor, the *Boston Globe–Horn Book* Award, and a *New York Times* Best Illustrated Book citation. He also won a Caldecott Honor for his art in THE RELATIVES CAME by Cynthia Rylant. Mr. Gammell lives in St. Paul, Minnesota.

Scary Stories 3

· ALSO BY ALVIN SCHWARTZ ·

And the Green Grass Grew All Around
Folk Poetry from Everywhere

Chin Music
Talk Talk and Other Talk

Cross Your Fingers, Spit in Your Hat
Superstitions and Other Beliefs

Flapdoodle
Pure Nonsense from American Folklore

More Scary Stories to Tell in the Dark

Scary Stories to Tell in the Dark

Stories to Tell a Cat

Tomfoolery
Trickery and Foolery with Words

A Twister of Twists, a Tangler of Tongues

Unriddling
All Sorts of Riddles to Puzzle Your Guessery, Collected from American Folklore

· I Can Read Books® ·
(for younger readers)

All of Our Noses Are Here
and Other Noodle Tales

Buzy Buzzing Bumblebees
and Other Tongue Twisters

Ghosts!
Ghostly Tales from Folklore

I Saw You in the Bathtub
and Other Folk Rhymes

In a Dark, Dark Room
and Other Scary Stories

Ten Copycats in a Boat
and Other Riddles

There Is a Carrot in My Ear
and Other Noodle Tales

Scary Stories 3

More Tales to Chill Your Bones

Collected from Folklore and Retold by

Alvin Schwartz

Drawings by Stephen Gammell

HarperCollins*Publishers*

Scary Stories 3: More Tales to Chill Your Bones
 Printed in the United States of America. For information address HarperCollins Children's Books, a division of HarperCollins Publishers, 1350 Avenue of the Americas, New York, NY 10019.

Library of Congress Cataloging-in-Publication Data
Schwartz, Alvin.

Scary Stories 3 : more tales to chill your bones / collected from folklore and retold by Alvin Schwartz ; drawings by Stephen Gammell.

p. cm.

Includes bibliographical references.

Summary: More traditional and modern-day stories of ghosts, haunts, superstitions, monsters, and horrible scary things.

ISBN 0-06-021794-4 — ISBN 0-06-021795-2 (lib. bdg.)

ISBN 0-06-440418-8 (pbk.)

1. Tales. 2. Ghost stories. 3. Horror tales. [1. Ghosts—Folklore. 2. Horror stories. 3. Folklore.] 1. Gammell, Stephen, ill. II. Title. II. Title: Scary stories three.

PZ8.1.S399Sb 1991 90-047474
398.2'5—dc20 CIP
AC

Visit us on the World Wide Web!
www.harperchildrens.com

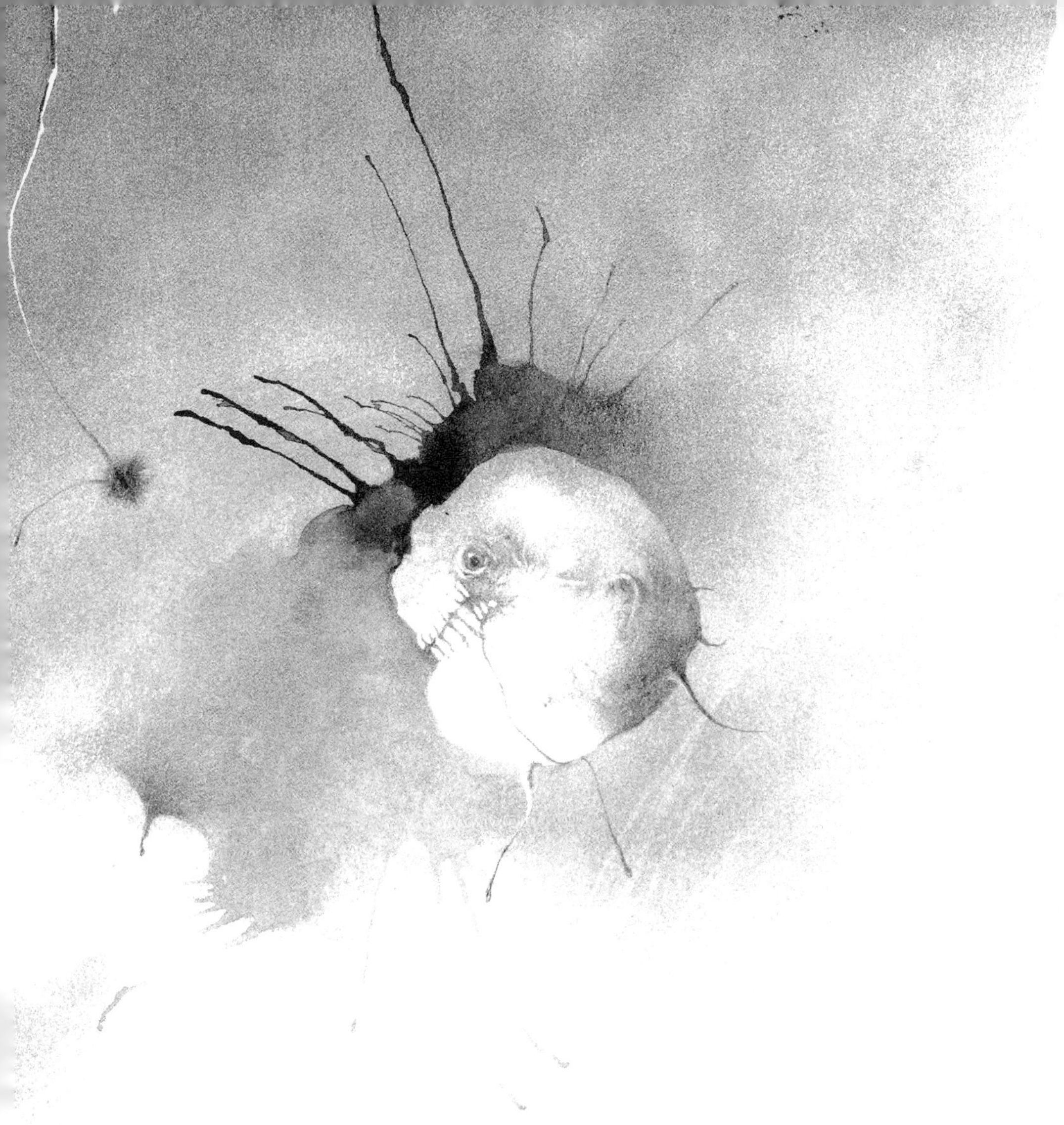

To Justin

Contents

Scary Stories 3

Boo Men

The girl was late getting home for supper. So she took a shortcut through the cemetery. But, oh, it made her nervous. When she saw another girl ahead of her, she hurried to catch up.

"Do you mind if I walk with you?" she asked. "Walking through the cemetery at night scares me."

"I know what you mean," the other girl said. "I used to feel that way myself when I was alive."

*

There are all sorts of things that scare us.

The dead scare us, for one day we will be dead like they are.

The dark scares us, for we don't know what is waiting in the dark. At night the sound of leaves rustling, or branches groaning, or someone whispering, makes us uneasy. So do footsteps coming closer. So do strange figures we think we see in the shadows—a human maybe, or a big animal, or some horrible thing we can barely make out.

People call these creatures we think we see "boo men." We imagine them, they say. But now and then a boo man turns out to be real.

Queer happenings scare us, too. We hear of a boy or a girl who was raised by an animal, a human being like us who yelps and howls and runs on all fours. The thought of it makes our flesh crawl. We hear of insects that make their nests in a person's body or of a nightmare that comes true, and we shudder. If such things really do happen, then they could happen to us.

It is from such fears that scary stories grow. This is the third book of such stories I have collected. I learned some of them from people I met. I found others, tales that had been written down, in folklore archives and in libraries. As we always do with tales we learn, I have told them in my own way.

Some stories in this book have been told only in recent times. But others have been part of our folklore for as long as we know. As one person told another, the details may have changed. But the story itself has not, for what once frightened people still frightens them.

I thought at first that one of the stories I found was a modern story. It is the one I call "The Bus Stop." I then discovered that a similar story had been told two thousand years earlier in ancient Rome. But the young woman involved was named Philinnion, not Joanna, as she is in our story.

Are the stories in this book true? The one I call "The Trouble" is true. I can't be sure about the others. Most may have at least a little truth, for strange things sometimes happen, and people love to tell about them and turn them into even better stories.

Nowadays most people say that they don't believe in ghosts and queer happenings and such. Yet they still fear the dead and the dark. And they still see boo men waiting in the shadows. And they still tell scary stories, just as people always have.

Alvin Schwartz

When Death Arrives

When Death arrives,
it usually is the end of the story.
But in these stories
it is only the beginning.

· *THE APPOINTMENT* ·

A sixteen-year-old boy worked on his grandfather's horse farm. One morning he drove a pickup truck into town on an errand. While he was walking along the main street, he saw Death. Death beckoned to him.

The boy drove back to the farm as fast as he could and told his grandfather what had happened. "Give me the truck," he begged. "I'll go to the city. He'll never find me there."

His grandfather gave him the truck, and the boy sped away. After he left, his grandfather went into town looking for Death. When he found him, he asked, "Why did you frighten my grandson that way? He is only sixteen. He is too young to die."

"I am sorry about that," said Death. "I did not mean to beckon to him. But I *was* surprised to see him here. You see, I have an appointment with him this afternoon—in the city."

· *THE BUS STOP* ·

Ed Cox was driving home from work in a rainstorm. While he waited for a traffic light to change, he saw a young woman standing alone at a bus stop. She had no umbrella and was soaking wet.

"Are you going toward Farmington?" he called.

"Yes, I am," she said.

"Would you like a ride home?"

"I would," she said, and she got in. "My name is Joanna Finney. Thank you for rescuing me."

"I'm Ed Cox," he said, "and you're welcome."

On the way they talked and talked. She told him about her family and her job and where she had gone to school, and he told her about himself. By the time they got to her house, the rain had stopped.

"I'm glad it rained," Ed said. "Would you like to go out tomorrow after work?"

"I'd love to," Joanna said.

She asked him to meet her at the bus stop, since it was near her office. They had such a good time, they went out many times after that. Always they would meet at the bus stop, and off they would go. Ed liked her more each time he saw her.

But one night when they had a date to go out, Joanna did not appear. Ed waited at the bus stop for almost an hour. "Maybe something is wrong," he thought, and he drove to her house in Farmington.

An older woman came to the door. "I'm Ed Cox," he said. "Maybe Joanna told you about me. I had a date with her tonight. We were supposed to meet at the bus stop near her office. But she didn't show up. Is she all right?"

The woman looked at him as if he had said something strange. "I am Joanna's mother," she said slowly. "Joanna isn't here now. But why don't you come in?"

Ed pointed to a picture on the mantel. "That looks just like her," he said.

"It did, once," her mother replied. "But that picture was taken when she was your age—about twenty years ago. A few days later she was waiting in the rain at that bus stop. A car hit her, and she was killed."

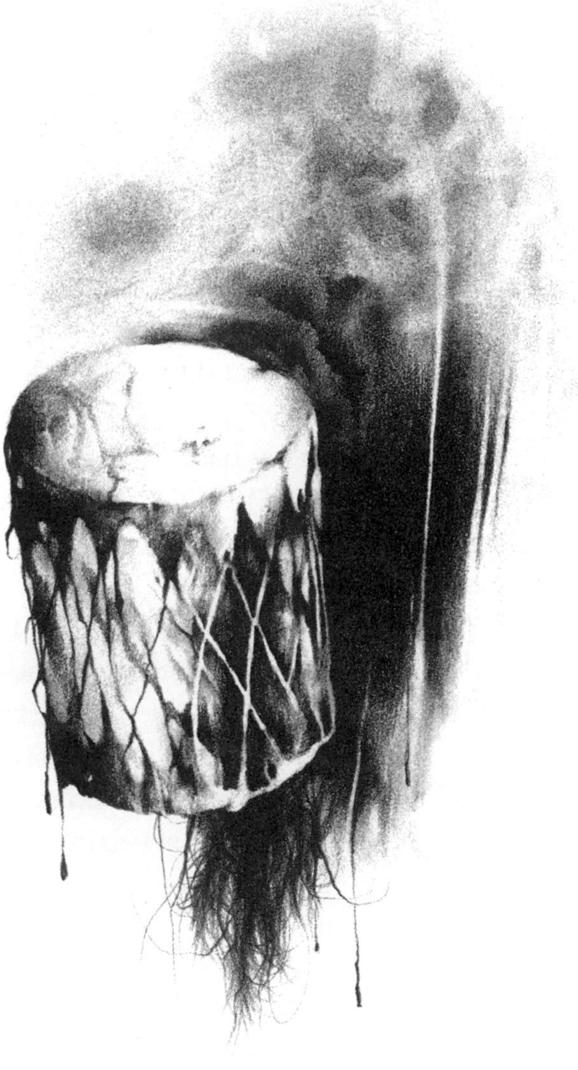

· *FASTER AND FASTER* ·

Sam and his cousin Bob went walking in the woods. The only sounds were leaves rustling and, now and again, a bird chirping. "It's so quiet here," Bob whispered.

But that soon changed. After a few minutes the two boys

started whooping and hollering and chasing one another around. Sam ducked behind a tree. When Bob came by, Sam jumped out at him. Then Bob raced ahead and hid behind a bush. When he looked down, there at his feet was an old drum.

"Sam! See what I found," he called. "It looks like a tom-tom. I bet it's a hundred years old."

"Look at the red stains on it," said Sam. "I bet it's somebody's blood. Let's get out of here."

But Bob could not resist trying the drum. He sat on the ground and held it between his legs. He beat on it with one hand, then the other, slowly at first, then faster and faster, almost as if he could not stop.

Suddenly there were shouts in the woods and the sound of hoofbeats. A cloud of dust rose from behind a line of trees. Then men on horseback galloped toward them.

"Bob! Let's go!" Sam shouted. He began to run. "Hurry!"

Bob dropped the drum and ran after him.

Sam heard the twang of a bow firing an arrow. Then he heard Bob scream. When Sam turned, he saw Bob pitch forward, dead. But there was no arrow in his body, and there was no wound. And when the police searched, there were no men on horseback, and there were no hoof-prints—and there was no drum.

The only sounds were leaves rustling and, now and again, a bird chirping.

· *JUST DELICIOUS* ·

George Flint loved to eat. Each day at noon he closed his camera shop for two hours and went home for a big lunch his wife Mina cooked for him. George was a bully, and Mina was a timid woman who did everything he asked because she was afraid of him.

On his way home for lunch one day, George stopped at the butcher shop and bought a pound of liver. He loved liver. He would have Mina cook it for dinner that night. Despite all his complaints about her, she was a very good cook.

While George ate his lunch, Mina told him that a rich old woman in town had died. Her body was in the church next door. It was in an open coffin. Anyone who wanted to see her could. As usual, George was not interested in what Mina had to say. "I've got to go back to work," he told her.

After he left, Mina began to cook the liver. She added vegetables and spices and simmered it all afternoon, just the way George liked it. When she thought it was done, she cut off a small piece and tasted it. It was delicious, the best she had ever made. She ate a second piece. Then a third. It was so good, she could not stop eating it.

It was only when the liver was all gone that she thought of George. He would be coming home soon. What would he do when he found that she had eaten all of the liver? Some men would laugh—but not George. He would be angry and mean, and she did not want to face that again. But where could she get another piece of liver that late in the day?

Then she remembered the old woman lying in the church next door waiting to be buried. . . .

George said he never had a better dinner. "Have some liver, Mina," he said. "It's just delicious."

"I'm not hungry," she said. "You finish it."

That night, after George had fallen asleep, Mina sat in bed trying to read. But all she could think about was what she had done. Then she thought she heard a woman's voice.

"Who has my liver?" it asked. "Who has it?"

Was it her imagination? Was she dreaming?

Now the voice was closer. "Who has my liver?" it asked. "Who has it?"

Mina wanted to run. "No, no," she whispered. "I don't have it. I don't have your liver."

Now the voice was right next to her. "Who has my liver?" it asked. "Who has it?"

Mina froze with terror. She pointed to George. "He does," she said. "*He* has it!"

Suddenly the light went out—and George screamed, and screamed.

· *HELLO, KATE!* ·

Tom Connors was on his way to a dance in the next village. It was a long walk through fields and woods. But it was a soft, sweet evening and he loved dancing, so Tom didn't mind.

He had gone only a short distance when he noticed a young woman following him. "Maybe she is going to the dance," he thought, and he stopped and waited for her. As the woman got closer, he saw that it was Kate Faherty. They had danced together many times.

He was about to call "Hello, Kate!" when suddenly he remembered that Kate was dead. She had died last year, yet there she was all dressed up for the dance. Tom wanted to run, but somehow it didn't seem right to run from Kate. He turned and started to walk away as fast as he could, but Kate followed him. He took a shortcut across a field, but still she followed.

When he got to the dance hall, she was right behind him. There were a lot of people standing outside, and Tom tried to lose Kate in the crowd. He worked his way to the side of the building, then squeezed up against the wall behind some people.

But Kate followed. She came so close she brushed up against him. Then she stopped and waited. He wanted to say "Hello, Kate!" just the way he did when she was alive. But he was so frightened he couldn't speak. Her eyes looked into his eyes—and she vanished.

· THE BLACK DOG ·

It was eleven o'clock at night. Peter Rothberg was in bed on the second floor of the old house where he lived alone. It had gotten so chilly, he went downstairs to turn up the heat.

As Peter was on his way back to bed, a black dog ran down the stairs. It passed him and disappeared into the darkness. "Where did *you* come from?" Peter said. He had never seen the dog before.

He turned on all the lights and looked in every room. He could not find the dog anywhere. He went outside and brought in the two watchdogs he kept in the backyard. But they acted as if they were the only dogs in the house.

The next night, again at eleven o'clock, Peter was in his bedroom. He heard what sounded like a dog walking around in the room above him. He dashed upstairs and threw open the door. The room was empty. He looked under the bed. He looked in the closet. Nothing. But when he got back to his bedroom, he heard a dog running down the stairs. It was the black dog. He tried to follow it, but again he could not find where it had gone.

From then on, every night at eleven, Peter heard the dog walking in the room above him. The room was always empty. But after he left, the dog would come out of hiding, run down the stairs, and disappear.

One night Peter's neighbor waited with him for the dog. At the usual time they heard it above them. Then they heard it on the stairs. When they went out into the hall, it was standing at the foot of the stairs looking up at them.

The neighbor whistled, and the dog wagged its tail. Then it was gone.

Things went on this way until the night Peter decided to bring his watchdogs into the house again. Maybe this time they would find the black dog and drive it away. Just before eleven he took them up to his bedroom and left the door open.

Then he heard the black dog moving around above him. His dogs pricked up their ears and ran to the door. Suddenly they bared their teeth and snarled and backed away. Peter could not see the black dog or hear it, but he was sure that it had entered his room. His dogs barked and snapped. They darted forward nervously, then backed away again.

Suddenly one of them yelped. It began bleeding, then dropped to the floor, its neck torn open. A minute later it was dead. Peter's other dog backed into a corner, whimpering. Then everything was still.

The next night Peter's neighbor came back with a pistol. Again they waited in his bedroom. At eleven o'clock the black dog came down the stairs. As before, it looked up at them and wagged its tail. When they started toward it with the pistol, it growled and disappeared.

That was the last Peter saw of the black dog. But it did not mean that the dog was gone. Now and then, always at eleven, he heard it moving around above him. Once he heard it running down the stairs. He never managed to see it again. But he knew that it was there.

· FOOTSTEPS ·

Liz was doing her homework at the dining-room table. Her younger sister Sarah was asleep upstairs. Their mother was out, but she was expected back any minute.

When the front door opened and shut, Liz called, "Hello, Mama!" But her mother didn't answer. And the footsteps Liz heard were heavier, like a man's.

"Who's there?" she called. No one replied. She heard whoever it was walk through the living room, then up the stairs to the second floor. The footsteps moved from one bedroom to another.

Again Liz called, "Who's there?" The footsteps stopped. Then she thought, "Oh, my God! Sarah is in her bedroom." She ran upstairs to Sarah's room. Only Sarah was there, and she was asleep. Liz looked in the other rooms, but found no one. She went back down to the dining room, scared out of her wits.

Soon she heard footsteps again. They were coming down the stairs, into the living room. Now they went into the kitchen. Then the door between the kitchen and the dining room slowly began to open. . . .

"Get out!" Liz screamed. The door slowly closed. The footsteps moved out of the kitchen, through the living room, toward the front door. The door opened and shut.

Liz ran to the window to see who it was. No one was in sight. Nor were there any footprints in the fresh snow that had been falling.

· *LIKE CATS' EYES* ·

As Jim Brand lay dying, his wife left him with his nurse and went into the next room to rest. She sat in the dark staring into the night. Suddenly Mrs. Brand saw headlights come rapidly up the driveway.

"Oh, no," she thought. "I don't want visitors now, not now." But it wasn't a car bringing a visitor. It was an old hearse with maybe a half dozen small men hanging from the sides. At least, that's what it looked like.

The hearse screeched to a stop. The men jumped off and stared up at her, their eyes glowing with a soft, yellow light, like cats' eyes. She watched with horror as they disappeared into the house.

An instant later they were back, lifting something into the hearse. Then they drove off at high speed, wheels squealing, the gravel in the driveway flying in all directions.

At that moment the nurse came in to say that Jim Brand had died.

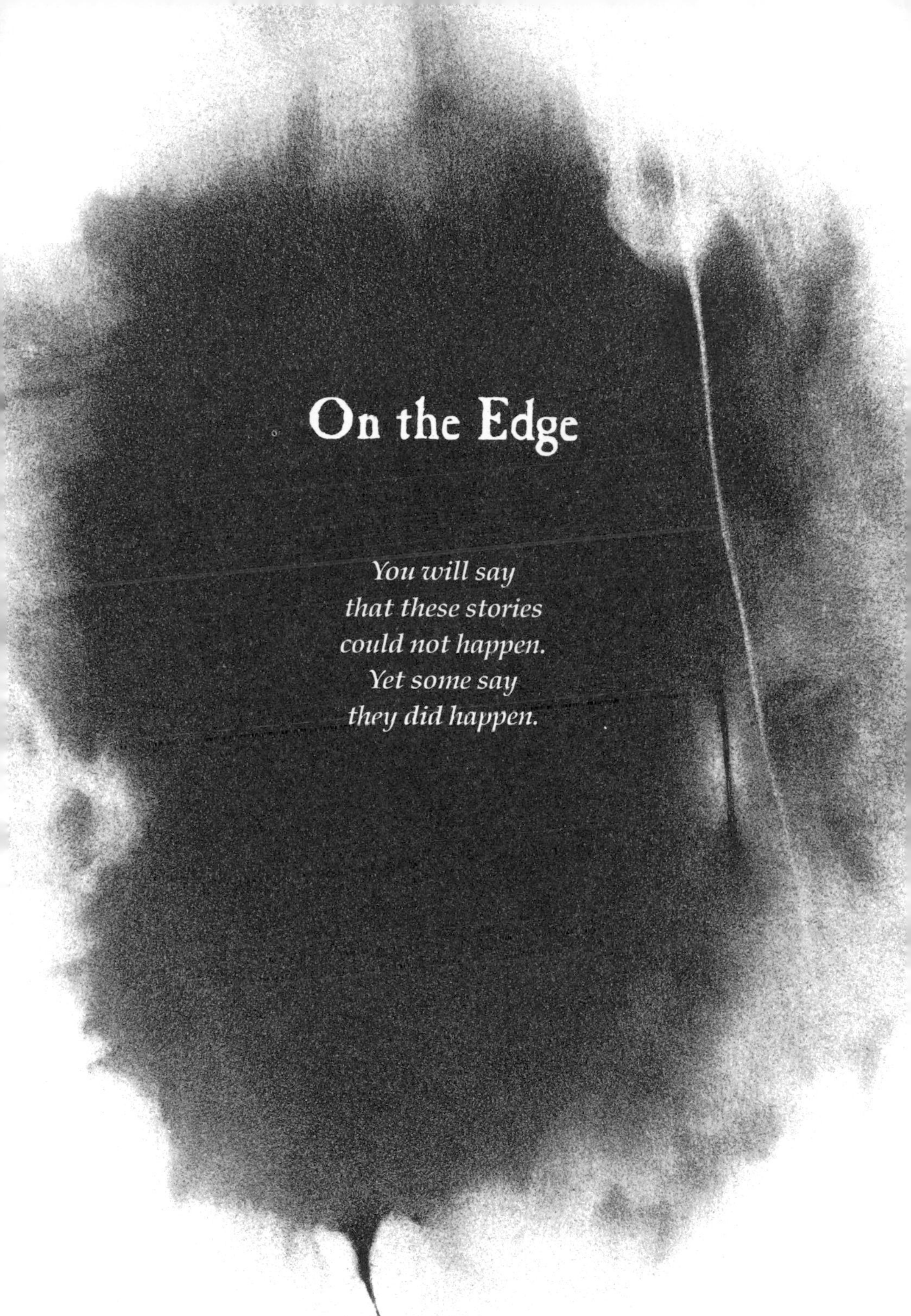

On the Edge

You will say
that these stories
could not happen.
Yet some say
they did happen.

· *BESS* ·

John Nicholas raised horses. He had many horses of all kinds, but his favorite was Bess, a gentle old mare he had grown up with. He no longer rode her, for all she could do now was just amble along. Bess spent her days grazing peacefully in a meadow.

That summer, for the fun of it, John Nicholas went into a fortune-teller's booth. The fortune-teller studied her cards. "I see danger ahead for you," she said. "Your favorite horse will cause you to die. I don't know when, but it will happen. It is in the cards."

John Nicholas laughed. The idea that Bess would cause his death was nonsense. She was as dangerous as a bowl of soup. Yet from then on, whenever he saw her, he remembered the fortune-teller's warning.

That fall a farmer from the other end of the county asked if he could have Bess. He had been thinking that the old horse would be perfect for his children to ride.

"That's a good idea," John said. "It would be fun for them, and it would give Bess something to do."

Later John told his wife about it. "Now Bess won't kill me," he said, and they both laughed.

A few months later, he saw the farmer who had taken her. "How's my Bess?" he asked.

"Oh, she was fine for a while," the farmer said. "The children loved her. Then she got sick. I had to shoot her to put her out of her misery. It was a shame."

Despite himself, John breathed a sigh of relief. He had often wondered if in some crazy way, through some

strange accident, Bess would kill him. Now, of course, she could not.

"I'd like to see her," said John. "Just to say good-bye. She was my favorite."

The bones of the dead horse were in a far corner of the man's farm. John kneeled down and patted Bess's sun-bleached skull. Just then a rattlesnake, which had made its home inside the skull, sank its fangs into John Nicholas's arm and killed him.

· *HAROLD* ·

When it got hot in the valley, Thomas and Alfred drove their cows up to a cool, green pasture in the mountains to graze. Usually they stayed there with the cows for two months. Then they brought them down to the valley again.

The work was easy enough, but, oh, it was boring. All day the two men tended their cows. At night they went

back to the tiny hut where they lived. They ate supper and worked in the garden and went to sleep. It was always the same.

Then Thomas had an idea that changed everything. "Let's make a doll the size of a man," he said. "It would be fun to make, and we could put it in the garden to scare away the birds."

"It should look like Harold," Alfred said. Harold was a farmer they both hated. They made the doll out of old sacks stuffed with straw. They gave it a pointy nose like Harold's and tiny eyes like his. Then they added dark hair and a twisted frown. Of course they also gave it Harold's name.

Each morning on their way to the pasture, they tied

Harold to a pole in the garden to scare away the birds. Each night they brought him inside so that he wouldn't get ruined if it rained.

When they were feeling playful, they would talk to him. One of them might say, "How are the vegetables growing today, Harold?" Then the other, making believe he was Harold, would answer in a crazy voice, "*Very* slowly." They both would laugh, but not Harold.

Whenever something went wrong, they took it out on Harold. They would curse at him, even kick him or punch him. Sometimes one of them would take the food they were eating (which they both were sick of) and smear it on the doll's face. "How do you like that stew, Harold?" he would ask. "Well, you'd better eat it—or else." Then the two men would howl with laughter.

One night, after Thomas had wiped Harold's face with food, Harold grunted.

"Did you hear that?" Alfred asked.

"It was Harold," Thomas said. "I was watching him when it happened. I can't believe it."

"How could he grunt?" Alfred asked. "He's just a sack of straw. It's not possible."

"Let's throw him in the fire," said Thomas, "and that will be that."

"Let's not do anything stupid," said Alfred. "We don't know what's going on. When we move the cows down, we'll leave him behind. For now, let's just keep an eye on him."

So they left Harold sitting in a corner of the hut. They didn't talk to him or take him outside anymore. Now and then the doll grunted, but that was all. After a few days they decided there was nothing to be afraid of. Maybe a mouse or some insects had gotten inside Harold and were making those sounds.

So Thomas and Alfred went back to their old ways. Each morning they put Harold out in the garden, and each night they brought him back into the hut. When they felt playful, they joked with him. When they felt mean, they treated him as badly as ever.

Then one night Alfred noticed something that frightened him. "Harold is growing," he said.

"I was thinking the same thing," Thomas said.

"Maybe it's just our imagination," Alfred replied. "We have been up here on this mountain too long."

The next morning, while they were eating, Harold stood up and walked out of the hut. He climbed up on the roof and trotted back and forth, like a horse on its hind legs. All day and all night long he trotted like that.

In the morning Harold climbed down and stood in a far corner of the pasture. The men had no idea what he would do next. They were afraid.

They decided to take the cows down into the valley that same day. When they left, Harold was nowhere in sight. They felt as if they had escaped a great danger and began joking and singing. But when they had gone only a mile or two, they realized they had forgotten to bring the milking stools.

Neither one wanted to go back for them, but the stools would cost a lot to replace. "There really is nothing to be afraid of," they told one another. "After all, what could a doll do?"

They drew straws to see which one would go back. It was Thomas. "I'll catch up with you," he said, and Alfred walked on toward the valley.

When Alfred came to a rise in the path, he looked back for Thomas. He did not see him anywhere. But he did see Harold. The doll was on the roof of the hut again. As Alfred watched, Harold kneeled and stretched out a bloody skin to dry in the sun.

· THE DEAD HAND ·

The village huddled on the edge of a vast swamp. As far as one could see, there were soggy meadows, holes filled with black water, and glistening sheets of wet, spongy peat. Skeletons of giant trees—"snags," the people called them—rose up out of the muck, their dead branches reaching out like long, twisted arms.

During the day, the men in the village cut the peat and hauled it home to dry and sell for fuel. But when the sun went down, and the wind, sighing and moaning, came in from the sea, the men were quick to leave. Strange creatures took over the swamp at night, and some even came into the village—that's what everyone said. People were so afraid, they would not go out alone after dark.

Young Tom Pattison was the only person in the village who did not believe in these creatures. On his way home from work, he'd whisper to his friends, "There's one!" and they would jump and run. And Tom would laugh and laugh.

Finally some of his friends turned on him. "If you know so much," they said, "go back into the swamp some night and see what comes of it."

"I'll do it," said Tom. "I work out there every day. Not once have I ever seen anything to frighten me. Why should it be different at night? Tomorrow night I'll take my lantern and walk out to the willow snag. If I get scared and run, I'll never make fun of you again."

The next night the men went to Tom Pattison's house to see him on his way. Thick clouds covered the moon. It was the blackest of nights. When they arrived, Tom's mother was pleading with him not to go.

"I'll be all right," he said. "There's nothing to be afraid of. Don't be foolish like the rest."

He took his lantern and, singing to himself, headed down the spongy path toward the willow snag.

Some of the young men wondered if Tom wasn't right. Maybe they were afraid of things that did not exist. A few decided to follow him and see for themselves, but they stayed far behind in case he ran into trouble. They were sure they saw dark shapes moving about. But Tom's lantern kept bobbing up and down, and Tom's songs kept floating back to them, and nothing happened.

Finally they caught sight of the willow snag. There was Tom standing in a circle of light, looking this way and that. All of a sudden the wind blew out his lantern, and Tom stopped singing. The men stood stock-still in the blackness, waiting for something awful to happen.

The clouds shifted and the moon came out. There was Tom again. Only now he had his back pushed up against the willow snag, and he had his arms out in front of him, as if he were fighting something off. From where the men stood, it looked like dark shapes were swirling in around him. Then the clouds covered the moon again. Once more it was as black as pitch.

When the moon came out again, Tom was hanging on to the willow snag with one arm. His other arm was stretched out in front of him, as if something was pulling it. It looked to the men as if a rotting, moldy hand with no arm—a dead hand—had grabbed Tom's hand. With one

final wrench, whatever had hold of Tom jerked him into the muck. That's what the men said.

When the clouds blotted out the moon once more, the men turned and ran through the blackness toward the village. Again and again they lost the path and fell into the muck and water holes. In the end they crawled back on their hands and knees. But Tom Pattison was not with them.

In the morning the people searched everywhere for Tom. Finally they gave him up for lost.

A few weeks later, toward evening, the villagers heard a cry. It was Tom's mother. She was rushing down the path from the swamp, shouting and waving. When she was sure the villagers had spotted her, she turned and ran back. Off they went after her.

They found young Tom Pattison by the willow snag, groaning and gibbering as if he had lost his mind. He kept pointing with one hand at something only he could see. Where his other hand should have been, there was nothing but a ragged stump oozing blood. The hand had been ripped clean off.

Everybody said it was the dead hand that had done it. But nobody really knows. Nobody will ever know—except Tom Pattison. And he never spoke another word again.

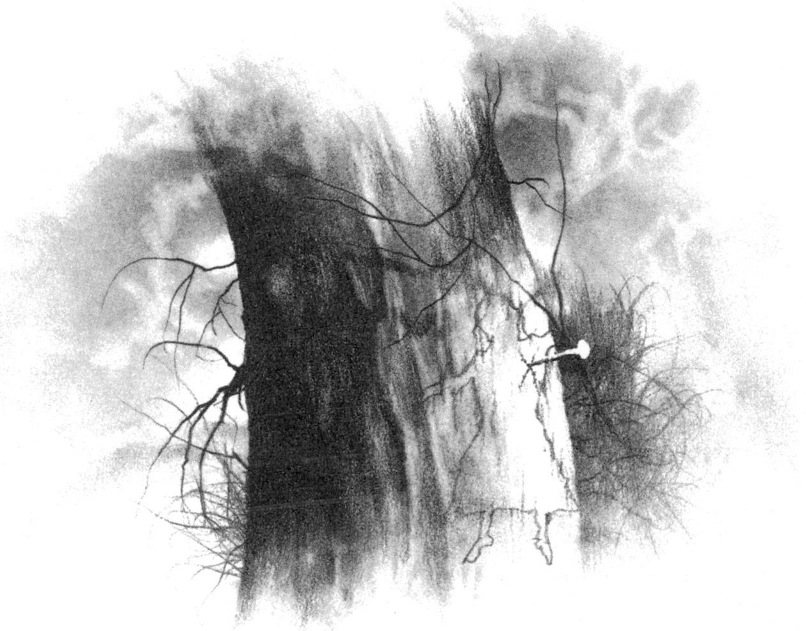

· *SUCH THINGS HAPPEN* ·

When Bill Nelson's cow stopped giving milk, he called the veterinarian. "There's nothing wrong with that cow," the vet said. "She's just stubborn. That, or some witch got hold of her." Bill and the vet both laughed.

"That old hag, Addie Fitch, I guess she's the closest we've got to a witch around here," the vet said. "But witches have gone out of style, haven't they?"

Bill had had a run-in with Addie Fitch the month before. He had hit her cat with his car and killed it. "I'm really sorry, Addie Fitch," he told her. "I'll get you a new cat, just as pretty, just as good."

Her eyes filled with hate. "I raised that cat from a kitten," she hissed. "I loved her. You'll be sorry for this, Bill Nelson."

Bill sent her a new cat and heard nothing more.

Then his cow stopped giving milk. Next his old truck broke down. After that, his wife fell and broke her arm. "We're having a lot of bad luck," he thought. Then he thought, "Maybe it is Addie Fitch gettin' even." And then, "Hey—you don't believe in witches. You're just upset."

But Bill's grandpa believed in witches. He had once told Bill that there was only one sure way to stop a witch from causing trouble. "You find a black walnut tree," he said, "and you draw her picture on it. Then you mark an *X* where her heart is, and you drive a nail into the *X*. Every day you drive it in a little deeper.

"If she's causing the trouble," he said, "she'll feel pain. When she can't stand it anymore, she'll come to you, or send somebody, and try to borrow something. If you give her what she wants, that breaks the power of the nail, and she'll go on tormenting you. But if you don't, she'll have to stop—or the pain will kill her."

That's what his nice, gentle old grandpa believed. "It's pure craziness," Bill thought. Of course, his grandpa didn't have much schooling. Bill had been to college. He knew better.

Then Bill's dog Joe, a perfectly healthy dog, dropped dead, just like that. It made Bill angry. Despite all his schooling, he thought, "Maybe it is Addie Fitch after all."

He got a red crayon from his son's room, and a hammer and a nail, and went into the woods. He found a black walnut tree and drew a picture of Addie Fitch on it. He made an *X* where her heart was, like his grandpa had said to do. With the hammer he drove the nail a little way into the *X*. Then he went home.

"I feel like a fool," he told his wife.

"You should," she said.

The next day a boy named Timmy Logan came by. "Addie Fitch isn't feeling well," he said. "She wonders if she could borrow some sugar from you."

Bill Nelson stared at Timmy in amazement. He took a deep breath. "Tell her I'm sorry, but I don't have any sugar right now," he said.

When Timmy Logan left, Bill went back to the walnut tree and drove the nail in another inch. The next day the boy came back. "Addie Fitch is pretty sick," he said. "She's wondering if you've got any sugar yet."

"Tell her I'm sorry," Bill Nelson said. "But I still don't have any."

Bill went out into the woods and drove the nail in another inch. The following day the boy was back. "Addie Fitch is getting sicker," he said. "She really needs some sugar."

"Tell her I still don't have any," Bill answered.

Bill's wife was angry. "You've got to stop this," she said. "If this mumbo jumbo works, it's like murder."

"I'll stop when she does," he said.

Toward dusk he stood in the yard staring at the ridge where the old lady lived, wondering what was going on up there. Then, in the half darkness, he saw Addie Fitch coming slowly down the hill toward him. With her

pinched, bony face and her old black coat, she did look like a witch. As she got closer, Bill saw that she could barely walk.

"Maybe I'm really hurting her," he thought. He ran to get his hammer to pull the nail out. But before he could leave, Addie Fitch was in the yard, her face twisted with rage.

"First you killed my cat," she said. "Then you wouldn't give me a bit of sugar when I needed it." She swore at him, and fell dead at his feet.

*

"I'm not surprised that she dropped dead that way," the doctor said later. "She was very old, maybe ninety. It was her heart, of course."

"Some people thought she was a witch," Bill said.

"I've heard that," the doctor said.

"Somebody I know thought Addie Fitch had witched him," Bill went on. "He drew a picture of her on a tree, then drove a nail into it to make her stop."

"That's an old superstition," the doctor said. "But people like us don't believe in that sort of thing, do we?"

Running Wild

A young child is stolen by wild animals.
For some reason
the animals raise the child instead of eating it.
It learns to make the sounds they make.
It learns to eat, run, and kill
the way they do.
After a while it only looks human.

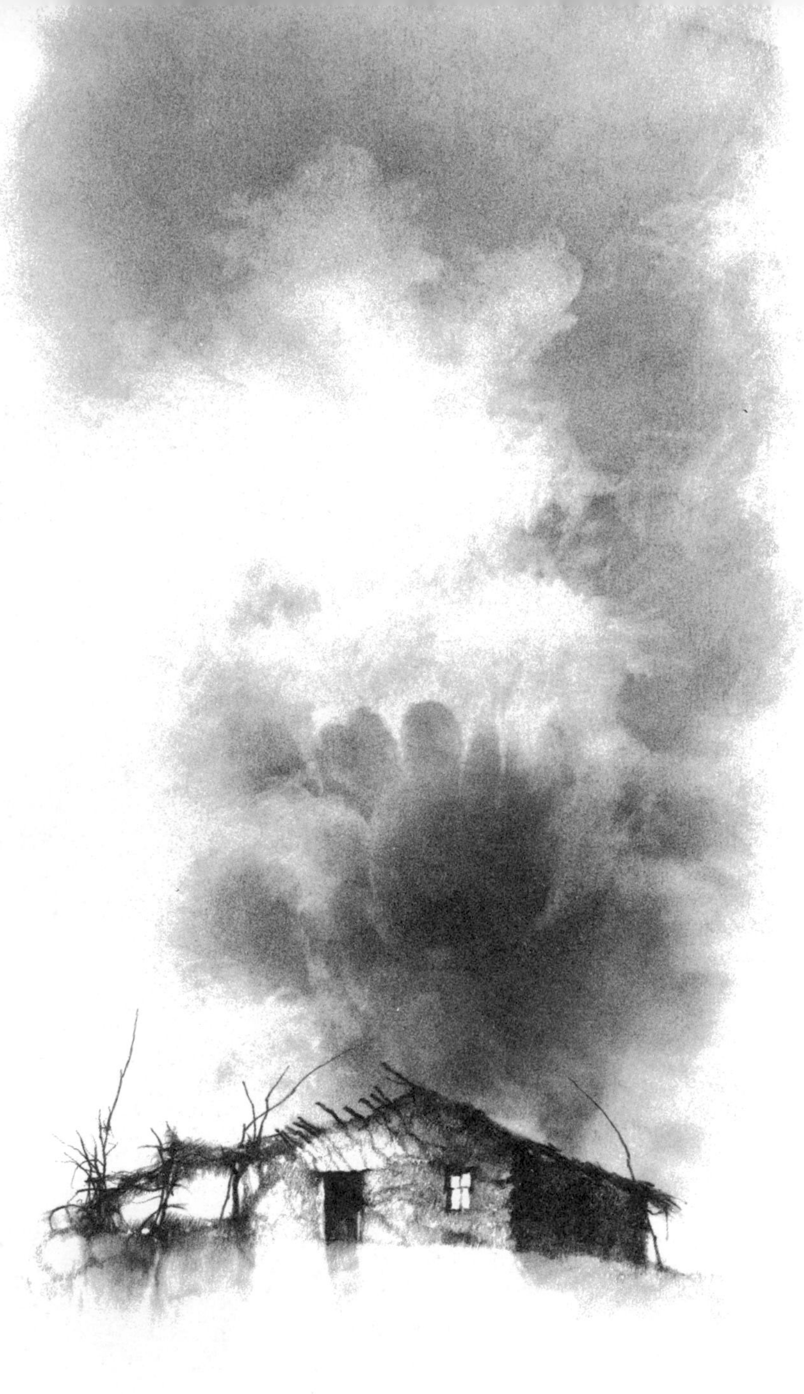

· *THE WOLF GIRL* ·

Travel northwest into the desert from Del Rio, Texas, and eventually you will come to Devil's River. In the 1830s a trapper named John Dent and his wife Mollie settled where Dry Creek runs into Devil's River. Dent was after beaver, which were plentiful there. He and Mollie built a cabin from brush, and near it they put up an arbor to give them shade.

Mollie Dent became pregnant. When she was ready to have their child, John Dent raced on horseback to their nearest neighbors, several miles away.

"My wife is having a baby," he said to the man and his wife. "Can you help us?" They agreed to come at once. As they got ready to leave, a violent storm came up and a bolt of lightning struck and killed John Dent. The man and his wife managed to find his cabin, but did not arrive until the next day. By then Mollie Dent was dead, too.

It looked as if she had given birth before she died, but the neighbors could not find the baby. Since there were wolf tracks all around, they decided the wolves had eaten it. They buried Mollie Dent and left.

A number of years after she died, people began to tell a strange tale. Some swore it was a true story. Others said it never could have happened.

*

The story begins in a small settlement a dozen miles from Mollie Dent's grave. Early one morning a pack of wolves raced in from the desert and killed some goats. Such attacks were not unusual in those days. But a boy thought he saw a naked young girl with long blond hair running with the wolves.

A year or two later, a woman came upon some wolves eating a goat they had just killed. Eating the goat with them, she claimed, was a naked young girl with long blond hair. When the wolves and the girl saw her, they fled. The woman said that at first the girl ran on all fours. Then she stood and ran like a human, swiftly as the wolves.

People started wondering if this "wolf girl" was Mollie Dent's daughter. Had a mother wolf carried her off the day she was born and raised her with her pups? If so, by now she would be ten or eleven years old.

As the story is told, some men began to look for the girl. They searched along the riverbanks and in the desert and its canyons. And one day, it is said, they found her, walking in a canyon with a wolf at her side. When the wolf ran off, the girl hid in an opening in one of the canyon walls.

When the men tried to capture her, she fought back, biting and scratching like an enraged animal. When they finally subdued her, she began screaming like a frightened young girl and howling like a frightened young wolf.

Her captors bound her with rope, put her across a horse, and took her to a small ranch house in the desert. They would turn her over to the sheriff the next day, they decided. They placed her in an empty room and untied her. Terror-stricken, she hid in the shadows. They left her and locked the door.

Soon she was screaming and howling again. The men thought they would go mad listening to her, but at last she stopped. When night fell, wolves began howling in the

distance. People say that each time they stopped, the girl howled in reply.

As the story goes, the cries of wolves came from every direction and got closer and closer. Suddenly, as if a signal had been given, wolves attacked the horses and other livestock. The men rushed into the darkness, firing their guns.

High up in the wall, in the room where they had left the girl, was a small window. A plank was nailed across it. She pulled the plank off, crawled through the window, and disappeared.

*

Years passed with no word of the girl. Then one day some men on horseback came around a bend in the Rio Grande not far from Devil's River. They claimed they saw a young woman with long blond hair feeding two wolf pups.

When she saw the men, she snatched up the pups and ran into the brush. They rode after her, but she quickly left them behind. They searched and searched, but found no trace of her. That is the last we know of the wolf girl. And it is there, in the desert, near the Rio Grande, that this story ends.

Five Nightmares

An artist painted some pictures.
A boy got a new pet.
A girl went on vacation.
Everything was normal.
Then nothing was.

· THE DREAM ·

Lucy Morgan was an artist. She had spent a week painting in a small country town and decided that the next day she would move on. She would go to a village called Kingston.

But that night Lucy Morgan had a strange dream. She dreamed that she was walking up a dark, carved staircase and entered a bedroom. It was an ordinary room except for two things. Thc carpet was made up of large squares that looked like trapdoors. And each of the windows was fastened shut with big nails that stuck up out of the wood.

In her dream Lucy Morgan went to sleep in that bedroom. During the night a woman with a pale face and black eyes and long black hair came into the room. She leaned over the bed and whispered, "This is an evil place. Flee while you can." When the woman touched her arm to hurry her along, Lucy Morgan awakened from her dream with a shriek. She lay awake the rest of the night trembling.

In the morning she told her landlady that she had decided not to go to Kingston after all. "I can't tell you why," she said, "but I just can't bring myself to go there."

"Then why don't you go to Dorset?" the landlady said. "It's a pretty town, and it isn't too far."

So Lucy Morgan went to Dorset. Someone told her she could find a room in a house at the top of the hill. It was a pleasant-looking house, and the landlady there, a plump, motherly woman, was as nice as could be. "Let's look at the room," she said. "I think you will like it."

They walked up a dark, carved staircase, like the one in Lucy's dream. "In these old houses the staircases are all the same," Lucy thought. But when the landlady opened the door to the bedroom, it was the room in her dream, with the same carpet that looked like trapdoors and the same windows fastened with big nails.

"This is just a coincidence," Lucy told herself.

"How do you like it?" the landlady asked.

"I'm not sure," she said.

"Well, take your time," the landlady said. "I'll bring up some tea while you think about it."

Lucy sat on the bed staring at the trapdoors and the big nails. Soon there was a knock on the door. "It's the landlady with tea," she thought.

But it wasn't the landlady. It was the woman with the pale face and the black eyes and the long black hair. Lucy Morgan grabbed her things and fled.

· SAM'S NEW PET ·

Sam stayed with his grandmother when his parents went to Mexico for their vacation. "We are going to bring you back something nice," his mother told him. "It will be a surprise."

Before they came home, Sam's parents looked for something Sam would like. All they could find was a beautiful sombrero. It cost too much. But that afternoon, while they were eating their lunch in a park, they decided to buy the sombrero after all. Sam's father threw what was left of their sandwiches to some stray dogs, and they walked back to the marketplace.

One of the animals followed them. It was a small, gray creature with short hair, short legs, and a long tail. Wherever they went, it went.

"Isn't he cute!" Sam's mother said. "He must be one of those Mexican Hairless dogs. Sam would love him."

"He's probably somebody's pet," Sam's father said.

They asked several people if they knew who its owners were, but no one did. They just smiled and shrugged their shoulders. Finally, Sam's mother said, "Maybe he's just a stray. Let's take him home with us. We can give him a good home, and Sam will love him."

It is against the law to take a pet across the border, but Sam's parents hid the animal in a box, and no one saw it. When they got home, they showed it to Sam.

"He's a pretty small dog," said Sam.

"He's a Mexican dog," his father said. "I'm not sure what kind. I think it's called a Mexican Hairless. We'll find out. But he's nice, isn't he?"

They gave the new pet some dog food. Then they washed it and brushed it and combed its fur. That night it slept on Sam's bed. When Sam awakened the next morning, his pet was still there.

"Mother," he called, "the dog has a cold." The animal's eyes were running, and there was something white around its mouth. Later that morning Sam's mother took it to a veterinarian.

"Where did you get him?" the vet asked.

"In Mexico," she said. "We think he's a Mexican Hairless. I was going to ask you about that."

"He's not a Hairless," the vet said. "He's not even a dog. He's a sewer rat—and he has rabies."

· *MAYBE YOU WILL REMEMBER* ·

Mrs. Gibbs and her sixteen-year-old daughter Rosemary arrived in Paris on a hot morning in July. They had been on a vacation and now were returning home. But Mrs. Gibbs did not feel well. So they decided to rest in Paris for a few days before going on.

The city was crowded with tourists. Still, they found a place to stay at a good hotel. They had a lovely room overlooking a park. It had yellow walls, a blue carpet, and white furniture.

As soon as they unpacked, Mrs. Gibbs went to bed. She looked so pale that Rosemary asked to have the hotel's doctor examine her. Rosemary did not speak French, but fortunately the doctor spoke English.

He took one look at Mrs. Gibbs and said, "Your mother is too sick to travel. Tomorrow I will move her to a hospital, but she needs a certain medicine. If you go to my home for it, it will save time." The doctor said he did not have a telephone right now. Instead, he would give Rosemary a note for his wife.

The hotel manager put Rosemary in a taxi and, in French, told the driver how to find the doctor's house. "It will take only a little while," he told her, "and the taxi will bring you back." But as the driver slowly drove up one street and down another, it seemed to take forever. At one point Rosemary was sure they had gone down the same street twice.

It took almost as long for the doctor's wife to answer the door, then get the medicine ready. As Rosemary sat on a bench in the empty waiting room, she kept thinking, "Why can't you hurry? Please hurry." Then she heard a telephone ring somewhere in the house. But the doctor had told her he didn't have a telephone right now. What was going on?

They drove back as slowly as they had come, crawling up one street and down another. Rosemary sat in the backseat filled with dread, her mother's medicine clutched in her hand. Why was everything taking so long?

She was sure the taxi driver was going in the wrong direction. "Are you going to the right hotel?" she asked. He didn't answer. She asked again, but still he didn't reply. When he stopped for a traffic light, she threw open the door and ran from the cab.

She stopped a woman on the street. The woman did not speak English, but she knew someone who did. Rosemary was right. They *had* been driving in the wrong direction.

When she finally got back to the hotel, it was early evening. She went up to the desk clerk who had given

them their room. "I'm Rosemary Gibbs," she said. "My mother and I are in Room 505. May I please have the key?"

The clerk looked at her closely. "You must be mistaken," he said. "There is another guest in that room. Are you sure you are in the right hotel?" He turned to help someone else. She waited until he was finished.

"You gave us that room yourself when we arrived this morning," she said. "How could you forget?"

He stared at her as if she had lost her mind. "You must be mistaken," he said. "I have never seen you before. Are you sure you are in the right hotel?"

She asked to see the registration card they had filled out when they arrived. "It's June and Rosemary Gibbs," she said.

The clerk looked in the file. "We have no card for you," he said. "You must be in the wrong hotel."

"The hotel doctor will know me," Rosemary replied. "He examined my mother when we arrived. He sent me for medicine she needs. I want to see him."

The doctor came downstairs. "Here is the medicine for my mother," Rosemary said, holding it out to him. "Your wife gave it to me."

"I have never seen you before," he said. "You must be in the wrong hotel."

She asked for the hotel manager who had put her in the taxi. Surely he would remember her. "You must be in the wrong hotel," he said. "Let me give you a room where you can rest. Then maybe you will remember where you and your mother are staying."

"I want to see our room!" Rosemary said, raising her

505

voice. "It's Room 505."

But it was nothing like the room she remembered. It had a double bed, not twin beds. The furniture was black, not white. The carpet was green, not blue. There was someone else's clothing in the closet. The room she knew had vanished. And so had her mother.

"This is not the room," she said. "Where is my mother? What have you done with her?"

"You are in the wrong hotel," the manager said patiently, as if he were speaking to a young child.

Rosemary asked to see the police. "My mother, our things, the room, they have all disappeared," she told them.

"Are you sure you are in the right hotel?" they asked.

She went to her embassy for help. "Are you sure it is the right hotel?" they asked.

Rosemary thought that she was losing her mind.

"Why don't you rest here for a while," they said. "Then maybe you'll remember..."

*

But Rosemary's problem was not her memory. It was what she did not know. *See page 102.*

· *THE RED SPOT* ·

While Ruth slept, a spider crawled across her face. It stopped for several minutes on her left cheek, then went on its way.

"What is that red spot on my cheek?" she asked her mother the next morning.

"It looks like a spider bite," her mother said. "It will go away. Just don't scratch it."

Soon the small red spot grew into a small red boil. "Look at it now," Ruth said. "It's getting bigger. It's sore."

"That sometimes happens," her mother said. "It's coming to a head."

In a few days the boil was even larger. "Look at it now," Ruth said. "It hurts and it's ugly."

"We'll have the doctor look at it," her mother said. "Maybe it's infected." But the doctor could not see Ruth until the next day.

That night Ruth took a hot bath. As she soaked herself, the boil burst. Out poured a swarm of tiny spiders from the eggs their mother had laid in her cheek.

· *NO, THANKS* ·

Thursday nights Jim worked as a stock boy in one of the malls out on the highway. By eight-thirty he was usually finished and he drove home.

But that night Jim was one of the last to leave. By the time he got out to the huge parking lot, it was almost empty. The only sounds were cars in the distance and his footsteps on the pavement.

Suddenly a man stepped out of the shadows. "Hey, mister," he called in a low voice. He held out his right hand. Balanced on the palm was the long, thin blade of a knife.

Jim stopped.

"Nice, sharp knife," the man said softly.

"Don't panic," Jim thought.

The man stepped toward him.

"Don't run," Jim told himself.

"Nice, sharp knife," the man repeated.

"Give him what he wants," Jim thought.

The man came closer. He held the knife up. "Cuts nice and easy," he said slowly. Jim waited. The man peered into his face. "Hey, man, only three dollars. Two for five. Nice present for your mama."

"No, thanks," Jim said. "She's got one." And he ran for his car.

What Is Going On Here?

When bottles began popping
and furniture began flying all over the house,
there were many explanations.
but none of them was right.
Then someone had a scary answer
that could involve you.

· *THE TROUBLE* ·

The events in this story took place in 1958 in a small white house in a suburb of New York City. The names of the people involved have been changed.

*

Monday, February 3. Tom Lombardo and his sister Nancy had just come home from school. Tom was going on thirteen. Nancy was fourteen. They were talking to their mother in the living room when they heard a loud POP! in the kitchen. It sounded like a cork had been pulled from a bottle of champagne.

But it was nothing like that. The cap on a bottle of starch had somehow come unscrewed, and the bottle had tipped over and spilled. Then bottles all over the house began popping—bottles of nail polish remover, shampoo, bleach, rubbing alcohol, even a bottle of holy water.

Each had a screw cap that took two or three full turns to open. But each had opened *by itself*—without any human help—then had fallen over and spilled.

"*What* is going on here?" Mrs. Lombardo asked. Nobody knew. But the popping soon stopped and everything went back to normal. It was just one of those crazy things, they decided, and put it out of their minds.

Thursday, February 6. Just after Tom and Nancy got home from school, six more bottles popped their caps. The next day, at about the same time, another six did.

Sunday, February 9. At eleven o'clock that morning Tom was in the bathroom brushing his teeth. His father was standing in the doorway talking to him. All of a sudden a bottle of medicine began moving across the vanity by itself and fell into the sink. At the same time a bottle of shampoo moved to the edge of the vanity and crashed to the floor. They watched, spellbound.

"I'd better call the police," Mr. Lombardo said. That afternoon a patrolman interviewed the family as bottles popped in the bathroom. The police assigned a detective named Joseph Briggs to the case.

Detective Briggs was a practical man. When something moved, he believed that a human or an animal had moved it, or that it moved because of a vibration or the wind or some other natural cause. He did not believe in ghosts.

When the Lombardos said they had nothing to do with what was going on, he thought that at least one of them was lying. He wanted to examine the house. Then he wanted to talk to some experts and find out what they thought.

Tuesday, February 11. The bottle of holy water that had opened a week before opened a second time and spilled. Two days later it spilled again.

Saturday, February 15. Tom, Nancy, and a relative were watching TV in the living room when a small porcelain statue rose up from a table. It flew three feet through the air, then fell to the rug.

Monday, February 17. A priest blessed the Lombardos' house to protect it against whatever was causing the trouble.

Thursday, February 20. While Tom was doing his homework at one end of the dining room table, a sugar bowl at the other end flew into the hall and crashed. Detective

Briggs saw it happen. Later a bottle of ink on the table flew into a wall and broke, spattering in all directions. Then another porcelain statue took off. It traveled twelve feet and smashed into a desk.

Friday, February 21. To get some peace, the Lombardos went to a relative's house for the weekend. While they were gone, everything at home was normal.

Sunday, February 23. When the Lombardos returned, another sugar bowl took off. It flew into a wall and smashed to smithereens. Later a heavy bureau in Tom's room toppled over. But no one was in the room when it happened.

Monday, February 24. By now Detective Briggs had talked to an engineer, a chemist, a physicist, and others. Some thought that vibrations in the house were causing the trouble. These could come from underground water, they said, or from high-frequency radio waves, or from sonic booms caused by airplanes. Others said that the electrical system was the cause, or downdrafts coming through the chimney. The popping of bottles was blamed on chemicals the bottles contained.

Tests showed that there were no vibrations in the house; there was nothing wrong with the electrical system; and there were no chemicals in the bottles that would make them pop.

Then *what* was causing the trouble? None of the experts knew. But every day the Lombardos received dozens of letters and telephone calls from people who thought they did know. Many believed that the house was haunted. They thought that a poltergeist was on the loose—the

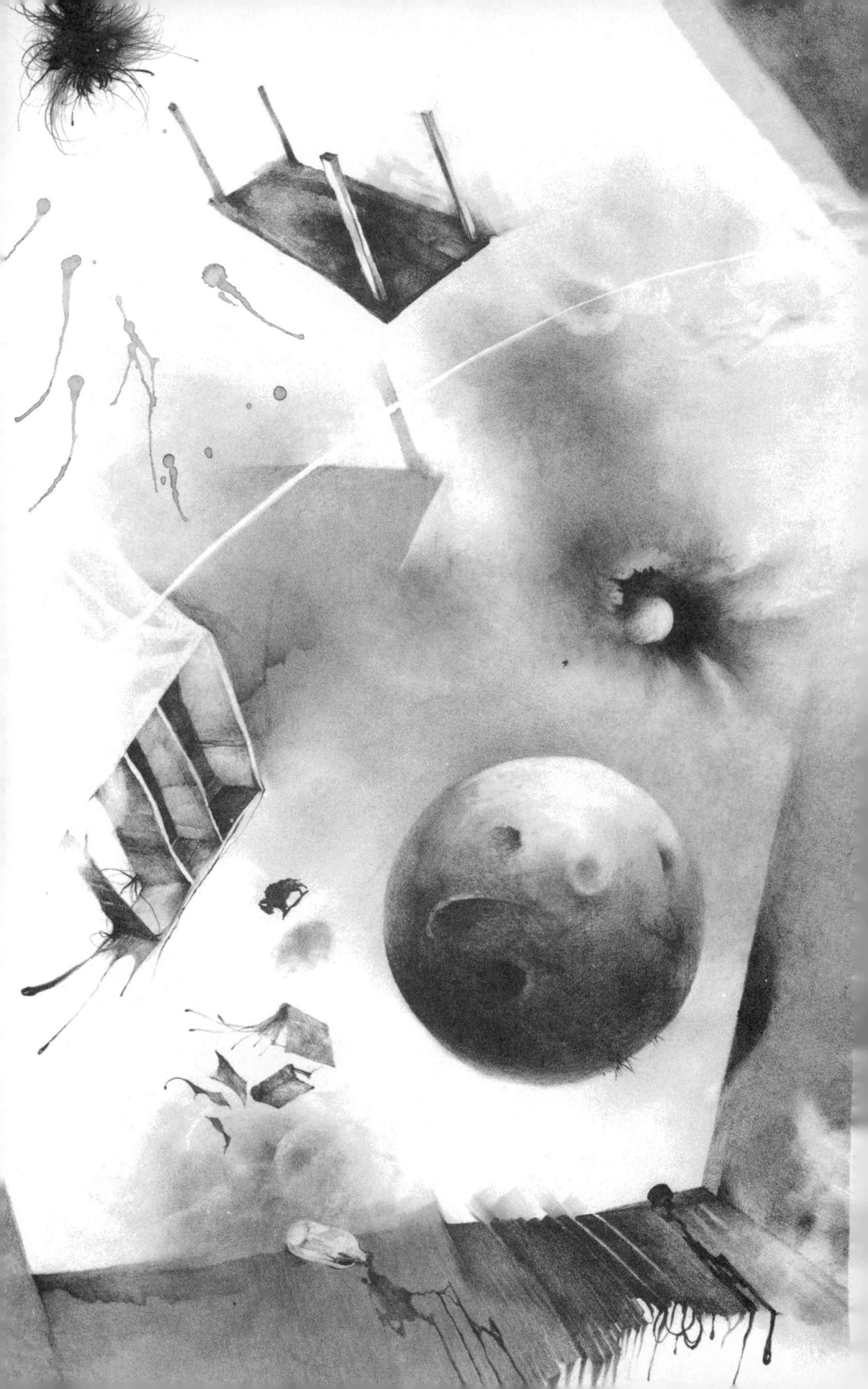

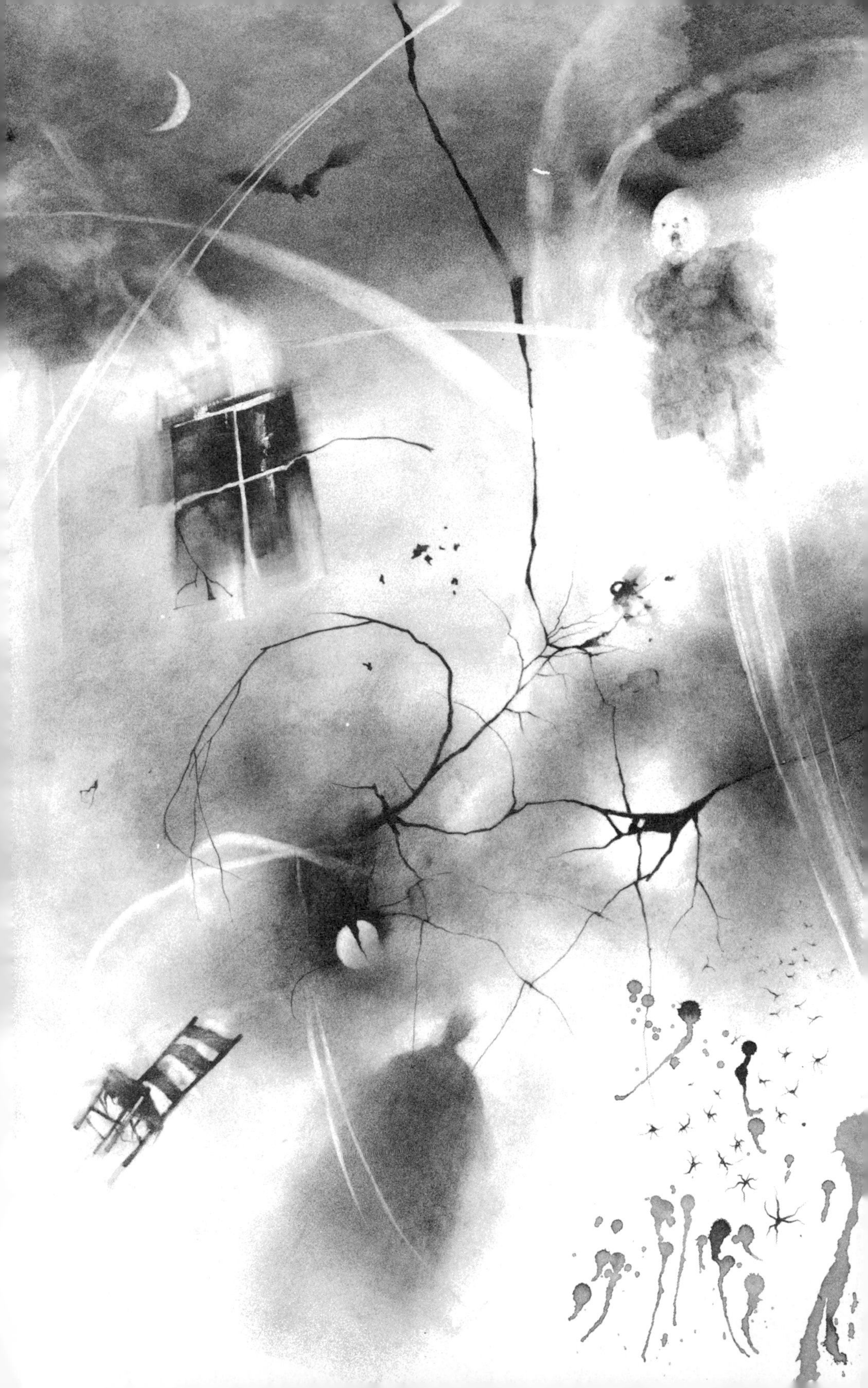

noisy ghost that is blamed when things move around on their own.

No one has proved that poltergeists exist. But people everywhere have told stories about them for hundreds of years. And what they have told was not too different from what was happening to the Lombardos.

Detective Briggs did not, of course, believe in poltergeists. He had begun to believe that Tom Lombardo might be to blame. Whenever something happened, Tom was usually in the room or nearby. When he accused Tom of causing the trouble, the boy denied it. "I don't know what's going on," he said. "All I know is that it scares me."

People said that Detective Briggs was a tough cop who would turn in his mother if she did something wrong. But he believed Tom. Only now he didn't know what to think.

Tuesday, February 25. A newspaper reporter came to the house to interview the family. Afterward he sat in the living room by himself hoping that something would happen that he could describe in his story.

Tom's room was just across the hall from where the reporter sat. The boy had gone to bed, but he had left his door open. Suddenly a globe of the world flew out of the darkened room and smashed into a wall. The reporter dashed into the bedroom and turned on the light. Tom was sitting in bed blinking, as if he had just been awakened from a sound sleep. "What was that?" he asked.

Wednesday, February 26. In the morning a small plastic statue of the Virgin Mary rose up from a dresser in Mr. and Mrs. Lombardo's bedroom and flew into a mirror. That night, while Tom was doing his homework, a ten-pound record player took off from a table, flew fifteen feet, then crashed to the floor.

Friday, February 28. Two scientists arrived from Duke University in North Carolina. They were parapsychologists who studied experiences like those the Lombardos were having. They spent several days talking to the family and examining the house, trying to understand what was going on and what was causing it. One night a bottle of bleach popped its top, but that was all that happened during their visit.

They did not tell the Lombardos about a theory they had that a poltergeist actually might be involved in such cases. According to this idea, poltergeists were not ghosts. They were normal teenagers. They had become so troubled by a problem that their emotions built up into a kind of vibration. Since it was taking place in their unconscious minds, they didn't even know it was happening. But the vibration somehow left their bodies and moved whatever it struck. It happened again and again until the problem had been solved.

Scientists had given this strange power a name. They called it "psychokinesis," the ability to move objects with mental power, or mind over matter. No one knew if this really could happen, or how to prove it. Yet most reports of poltergeists did involve families with teenage children, and there were two teenagers in the Lombardo family.

Monday, March 3. The parapsychologists said that they would prepare a report on what they had learned. The day after they left the trouble returned with a vengeance.

Tuesday, March 4. In the afternoon a bowl of flowers flew

off the dining-room table and smashed into a cupboard. Then a bottle of bleach jumped out of a cardboard box and popped its top. Then a bookcase filled with encyclopedias fell over and wedged itself between a radiator and a wall. Then a flashlight bulb on a table rose up and hit a wall twelve feet away. Finally, four knocks were heard coming from the kitchen when nobody was in that room.

Wednesday, March 5. While Mrs. Lombardo was making breakfast, she heard a loud crash in the living room. The coffee table had turned over by itself. But that was the end of it. After a month of chaos everything returned to normal.

*

In August the two parapsychologists gave their report. They decided that the Lombardos had not made up the story. Nor had they imagined it. Their trouble had been real. But what had caused it?

They said that no pranks or tricks were involved, nor was any magic. As the police had done, they also ruled out vibrations from underground water and other physical causes.

The only explanation they could not rule out was the possibility that a teenage poltergeist had been at work, moving objects with mental power. They did not have enough evidence to prove it, but it was the only answer they had.

If it was a poltergeist, they thought it was Tom. If they were right, if a normal boy like Tom had become a poltergeist, this also might happen to other teenagers. It might even happen to you.

Whoooooooo?

There are four ghosts,
a ghostly monster,
and a corpse in this chapter.
But the stories about them
are funny,
not scary.

· *STRANGERS* ·

A man and a woman happened to sit next to one another on a train. The woman took out a book and began reading. The train stopped at a half dozen stations, but she never looked up once.

The man watched her for a while, then asked, "What are you reading?"

"It's a ghost story," she said. "It's very good, *very* spooky."

"Do you believe in ghosts?" he asked.

"Yes, I do," she replied. "There are ghosts everywhere."

"I don't believe in them," he said. "It's just a lot of superstition. In all my years I've never seen a ghost, not one."

"Haven't you?" the woman said—and vanished.

· THE HOG ·

When Arthur and Anne were in high school, they fell in love. They were both big, fat, and jolly and seemed suited to one another. But as sometimes happens, things didn't work out.

Arthur moved away and married someone else, and Anne didn't marry anyone. And not too many years later, she got sick and died. Some said it was from a broken heart.

One day Arthur was driving to a small town not far from where he and Anne had grown up. Soon he realized that a hog was following him. No matter how fast Arthur drove, the hog stayed right behind. Each time he looked back, there was the hog. It began to irritate him.

Finally he couldn't stand it any longer. He stopped his car and rapped the hog on its snout good and hard. "Get out of here, you fat, dirty thing!" he shouted.

To his astonishment, the hog spoke to him, and it was Anne's voice he heard. "It's her ghost!" he thought. "She has come back as a hog!"

"I was doing no harm, Arthur," the hog said. "I was just out for a brisk walk, enjoying myself. How could you strike me after all that we meant to one another?" With that, she turned and trotted away .

*

(When you tell this story, have the hog speak in a high voice.)

· IS SOMETHING WRONG? ·

A car broke down late at night way out in the country. The driver remembered passing an empty house a few minutes earlier. "I'll stay there," he thought. "At least I'll get some sleep."

He found some wood in the corner of the living room and made a fire in the fireplace. He covered himself with his coat and slept. Toward morning the fire went out, and the cold awakened him. "It'll be light soon," he thought. "Then I'll go for help."

He closed his eyes again. But before he could doze off there was a terrible crash. Something big and heavy had fallen out of the chimney. It lay on the floor for a minute. Then it stood up and stared down at him.

The man took one look and started running. He had never seen anything so horrible in his life. He paused just long enough to jump through a window. Then he ran, and ran, and ran—and ran until he thought his lungs would burst.

As he stood in the road panting, trying to catch his breath, he felt something tap him on the shoulder. He turned and found himself staring into two big, bloody eyes in a grinning skull. It was the horrible thing!

"Pardon me," it said. "Is something wrong?"

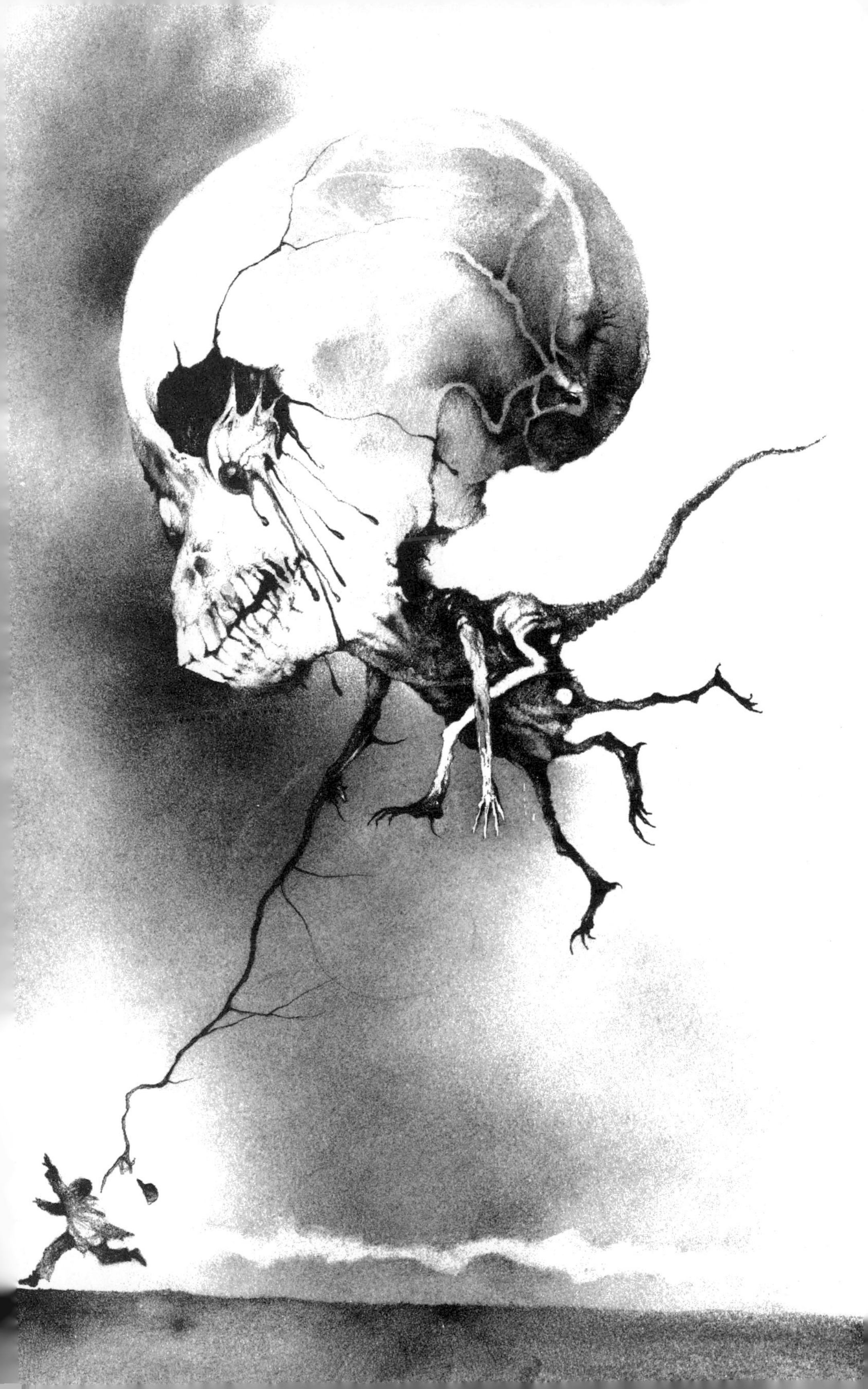

· *IT'S HIM!* ·

The woman was the meanest, most miserable person you could imagine. And her husband was just as bad. The only good thing was that they lived in the woods all by themselves and couldn't bother anybody else.

One day they were off somewhere getting firewood, and the woman got so mad at her husband that she grabbed an ax and cut his head off, just like that. Then she buried him nice and neat and went home.

She made herself a cup of tea and went out on the porch. She sat there rocking in her rocking chair, sipping her tea, thinking how glad she was that she had done this awful thing. After a while she heard this old, empty voice out in the distance moaning and groaning, and it was saying:

"Whoooooooo's going to stay with me this cold and lonely night? Whoooooooo?"

"It's *him!*" she thought. And she hollered back, "Stay by yourself, you old goat."

Soon she heard the voice again, only now it was closer, and it was saying:

"Whoooooooo's going to sit with me this cold and lonely night? Whoooooooo?"

"Only a crazy man!" she shouted. "Sit by yourself, you dirty rat!"

Then she heard the voice even closer, and it was saying:

"Whoooooooo's going to be with me this cold and lonely night? Whoooooooo?"

"Nobody!" she sneered. "Be by yourself, you miserable mole!"

She stood up to go into the house, but now the voice was right behind her, and it was whispering:

"Whoooooooo's going to stay with me this cold and lonely night? Whoooooooo?"

Before she could answer back, a big hairy hand came around the corner and grabbed her, and the voice hollered:

"*YOU* ARE!"

*

(As you say the last line, grab one of your friends.)

· *T-H-U-P-P-P-P-P-P-P!* ·

After Sarah went to bed, she saw a ghost. It was sitting on her dresser staring at her through two black holes where its eyes had been. She shrieked, and her mother and father came running.

"There's a ghost on my dresser," she said, trembling. "It's staring at me."

When they turned on the light, it was gone. "You were having a bad dream," her father said. "Now go to sleep."

But after they left, there it was again, sitting on her dresser staring at her. She pulled the blanket over her head and fell asleep.

The next night the ghost was back. It was up on the ceiling staring down at her. When Sarah saw it, she screamed. Again her mother and father came running.

"It's up on the ceiling," she said.

When they turned on the light, nothing was there. "It's your imagination," her mother said, and gave her a hug.

But after they left, there it was again, staring down at her from the ceiling. She put her head under the pillow and fell asleep.

The next night the ghost was back. It was sitting on her bed staring at her. Sarah called to her parents, and they came running.

"It's on my bed," she said. "It's looking and looking at me."

When they turned on the light, nothing was there. "You're upset over nothing," her father said. He kissed her on the nose and tucked her in. "Now go to sleep."

But after they left, there it was again, sitting on her bed staring at her.

"Why are you doing this to me?" Sarah asked. "Why don't you leave me alone?"

The ghost put its fingers in its ears and wiggled them at her. Then it stuck its tongue out and went:

"T-H-U-P-P-P-P-P-P-P!"

*

(To make this sound, put your tongue between your lips and blow. It is called giving someone "the raspberry.")

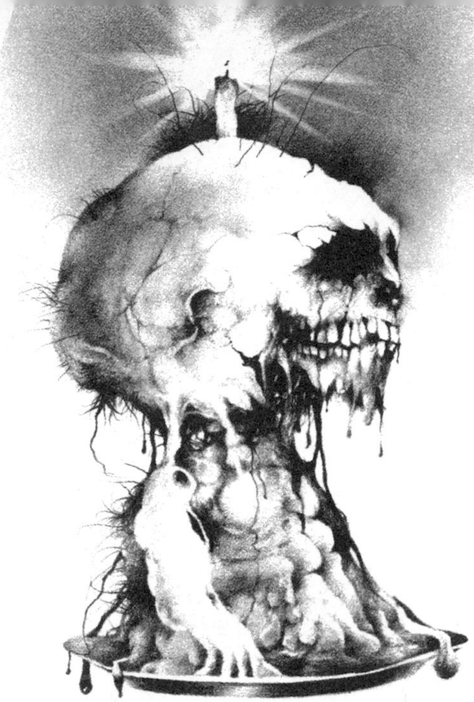

· *YOU MAY BE THE NEXT . . .* ·

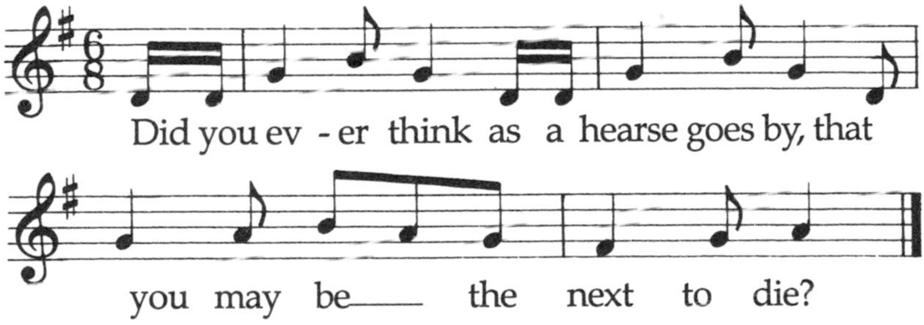

Did you ever think as a hearse goes by
That you may be the next to die?
They wrap you up in a big white sheet
From your head down to your feet.
And the worms crawl in and the worms crawl out,
In your stomach and out your snout,
And your eyes fall out and your teeth decay—
And that is the end of a perfect day.

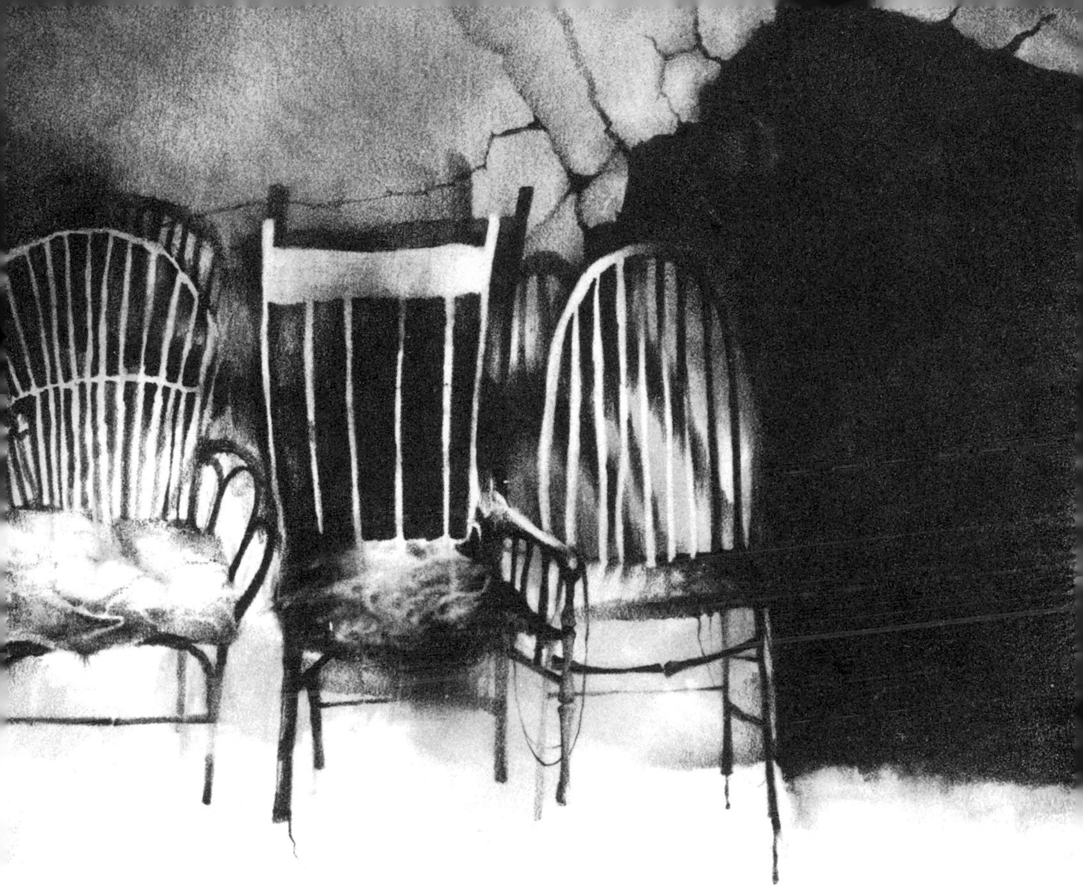

NOTES and SOURCES

BIBLIOGRAPHY

ACKNOWLEDGMENTS

Notes and Sources

The sources given are described in the Bibliography.

BOO MEN

"Boo men" is a name for imaginary scary creatures in Newfoundland. Boo men are similar to bogarts in Great Britain, from where many Newfoundlanders came, and to bogey men and boogeymen in America. See Widdowson, *If You Don't Be Good,* pp. 157–60; Widdowson, "The Bogeyman."

The story about the girl who meets a ghost in a cemetery is told in many places.

WHEN DEATH ARRIVES

The Appointment: This story is the retelling of an ancient tale that is usually set in Asia. A young man sees Death in the marketplace in Damascus, the capital of Syria. To escape his fate, he flees to either Baghdad or Samarra in what is now Iraq. Death is, of course, waiting for him. In some versions, Death is a woman, not a man. The story has been told in one form or another by Edith Wharton, the English author W. Somerset Maugham, and the French writer Jean Cocteau. The American novelist John O'Hara entitled his first book *An Appointment in Samarra.* See Woollcott, pp. 602–3.

The Bus Stop: This is from the family of "vanishing hitchhiker" stories in which a ghost returns in human form. It usually is seen on a street corner late at night or during a storm and is offered a ride home in a car. But when the driver arrives at his destination, the passenger has disappeared. In the story "The Bus Stop," the ghost remains in human form for several weeks before disappearing.

The story is based on several versions. One is a recollection by Barbara Carmer Schwartz from the 1940s in Delmar, New York. There also is a version in which the young man loses his mind when he learns that the young woman is a ghost. See Jones, *Things That Go Bump in the Night*, pp. 173–74.

A similar story was told in ancient Rome. It involved a young woman named Philinnion who died, then six months later was seen with a man she loved who did not know of her death. When her parents learn of her appearance, they rush to see her. She accuses them of interfering in her "life," then dies a second time. See Collison-Morley, pp. 652–72.

The folklorist Jan Brunvand lists many variants of the vanishing hitchhiker tale in *The Vanishing Hitchhiker,* pp. 24–40, 41–46.

There also have been at least two popular songs on the subject: "Laurie (Strange Things Happen)," a pop-rock song of the early 1960s composed by Milton C. Addington, and "Bringing Mary Home," a bluegrass song composed in 1961 by Joe Kingston and M. K. Scosa. Both were still being performed when this book was written.

Faster and Faster: This is retold from a summer-camp story of the 1940s in New York or New Hampshire. Ruth L. Tongue prints an account she collected in 1964 in Berkshire, England, in which some city boys find an old hunting horn in Windsor Forest. When one of them blows it, he summons up the ghosts of a hunting party and is killed by the ghostly arrows of a ghostly hunter. See Tongue, p. 52.

Just Delicious: This is one of hundreds of stories that make up what folklorists call the "Man from the Gallows" family, or tale type 366. They are found in America, Great Britain, Western Europe, and parts of Africa and Asia. Perhaps the best known in the English-speaking world is "The Man with the Golden Arm." For a version, see

Schwartz, *Tomfoolery*, pp. 28–30.

Such stories have their roots in the ancient tale of the man with no work whose family was starving. Searching for food, he comes to a gallows where a criminal has just been hanged. He cuts out the dead man's heart (or some other part of his body) and takes it home. That night his family feasts. But while they sleep, the man from the gallows comes looking for the part of his body that had been stolen. When he cannot find it, he takes with him the person who stole it. See Thompson, *The Folktale*, p. 42.

"Just Delicious" is a story that closely follows this tale. The retelling is based on accounts I have heard over the years in the northeastern United States, the earliest in the 1940s. Louis C. Jones prints a New York City version in which the husband saves himself by removing his wife's liver and giving it to the ghost as a substitute for the one she had stolen. See Jones, *Things That Go Bump in the Night*, pp. 96–99.

Hello, Kate!: This story is based on a legend from southwest Munster, Ireland. See Curtin, pp. 59–60.

The Black Dog: The story is based on an experience reported in the French village of Bourg-en-Forêt in the 1920s. A spectral black dog like the one in this story is said to be the ghost of a wicked human or a foreteller of death. See Van Paassen, pp. 246–50.

Footsteps: This story is loosely based on one collected in Amherst, Nova Scotia, by the Canadian folklorist Helen Creighton. See Creighton, pp. 264–66.

Like Cats' Eyes: This is adapted from a story the English author Augustus Hare was told in the late nineteenth century. In that version the hearse was pulled by four horses. See Hare, pp. 49–50.

ON THE EDGE

Bess: This story is based on an old European legend. The Swiss folklorist Max Lüthi named it "Oleg's Death" for the ruler Oleg, who lived almost two thousand years ago in what today is Russia. He is said to have died as John Nicholas did in our story, bitten by a poisonous snake hiding in the remains of a horse he feared.

The legend contains many themes that are frequently found in folk literature: What seems weak may be strong, what seems impossible may be possible, the greatest danger we face is from ourselves. See Lüthi, "Parallel Themes."

Harold: Several tales in folklore and fiction tell of a doll or some other figure a person creates that comes to life. In the Jewish legend of the golem, a rabbi uses a charm to give life to a clay statue. When it goes out of control, he destroys it. In Mary Wollstonecraft Shelley's novel *Frankenstein*, a Swiss student discovers how to bring lifeless matter alive and is destroyed by the monster he creates.

In the Greek fairy tale "The Gentleman Made of Groats," or "Mr. Simigaldi," a princess cannot find herself a good husband. So she creates one by mixing a kilo of almonds, a kilo of sugar, and a kilo of groats, which is similar to grits, and gives the mixture the shape of a man. In answer to her prayers, God gives the figure life. After many adventures, the two live happily.

The story "Harold" is retold from an Austrian-Swiss legend. See Lüthi, *Once Upon a Time*, pp. 83–87.

The Dead Hand: This legend was told in Lincolnshire in eastern England in the nineteenth century. It takes place in the Lincolnshire Cars, then a vast marshland on the North Sea that local people believed was a home to evil spirits. The story is shortened and adapted from M. C. Balfour, pp. 271–78.

Such Things Happen: This is a traditional American legend in which a person believes he is being tormented by a witch and tries to stop her. In some stories the person tries to kill the witch by drawing her picture and firing a silver bullet into it or by hammering a nail into it. I adapted and expanded this theme to point up the conflict between education and superstition that may arise when an educated person feels that events are out of control. See in Thompson, "Granny Frone," *Folk Tales and Legends*, pp. 650–52; Cox, pp. 208–9; Randolph, *Ozark Magic*, pp. 288–90; Yarborough, p. 97.

RUNNING WILD

The Wolf Girl: This legend from southwest Texas about a child who grew up wild is similar to stories found in many cultures. Some are described below.

I first heard about the Texas wolf girl in 1975 while in El Paso doing research for another book. A retired laborer then in his eighties, Juan de la Cruz Machuca, told me the story as he knew it. His version overlaps the account in "The Lobo Girl of Devil's River," an article on the history of the incident by L. D. Bertillion, that appeared in 1937. See Bertillion, pp. 79–85. My retelling is drawn from oral accounts and that article.

Bertillion begins his story when the trapper Dent falls in love with Mollie Pertul in Georgia, then soon after kills his partner in a trapping business and escapes. A year later he returns for Mollie and the two steal away to Texas and settle on Devil's River. There Mollie gives birth to their child who, in legend, became known as the wolf girl.

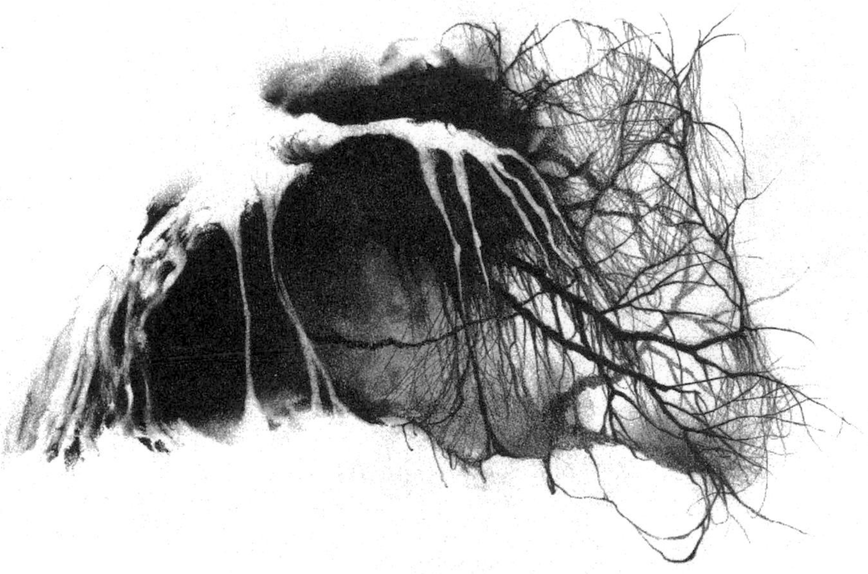

Sections of Devil's River and the Rio Grande where the wolf girl is said to have roamed have in modern times been flooded for a reservoir and recreation area.

One of the oldest legends of children who are raised by wolves is the famous story of the newborn twins Romulus and Remus, whose mother was said to have set them afloat in a basket on the Tiber River in ancient Latium. When the basket washed ashore, the boys were suckled by a she-wolf until a shepherd came upon them and raised them. In legend, Romulus founded Rome where the twins had been rescued from the Tiber.

In the story "Mowgli's Brother," Rudyard Kipling writes of a baby boy in India who walked into a den of wolves and was raised by them. See Kipling, pp. 1–43.

A modern legend from the Ozark Mountains in Arkansas tells of a five-month-old boy who disappeared when his mother placed him on the ground while she was hoeing corn with her husband. Years later some person or animal began stealing chickens from their farm, but the couple could not put a stop to it. One night the husband saw a naked boy run off with a chicken. When he followed the boy to a cave, he found him with an old, sick she-wolf that was eating the chicken. The boy growled at the farmer like a wolf, but the farmer managed to carry him off. It was, of course, his son. See Parler, p. 4.

There also are stories about young people who grew up wild after their parents had abandoned them, or after they had gotten lost or had been cast away. One is the true story of the wild boy of Aveyron who lived on his own in the wilderness in southern France from about 1795 to 1800, when he was captured. See Shattuck.

There are two California legends of such cases. One involves a two-year-old girl who washed ashore on an island off Santa Barbara after a sailboat swamped in the early 1900s. Years later men hunting wild goats on the island came upon a young woman who bounded away like a goat. They found her cowering at the back of a cave filled with bones of animals she had eaten. As the story goes, they took her to the mainland, where she was identified as the missing girl. There is no record of what happened to her. See Fife, p. 150.

The other legend is of a Native American girl who was left behind when her tribe abandoned San Nicholas Island seventy miles off Santa Barbara in 1835. She is said to have lived alone for eighteen years until she was rescued. The novel by Scott O'Dell, *Island of the Blue Dolphins,* is based on the story. See Ellison, pp. 36–38, 77–89; O'Dell.

FIVE NIGHTMARES

The Dream: Some dreams come true because it is logical that they do so. For examples see Schwartz, *Telling Fortunes,* pp. 57–64. But this dream is a puzzle. The story is based on an experience reported by Augustus Hare in his autobiography, p. 302.

Sam's New Pet: I heard this story in Portland, Oregon, in 1987. It was one of many versions being told in that period. Folklorist Jan Brunvand entitled one of his collections of modern legends *The Mexican Pet.* In it he reprints a 1984 variant of this story from Newport Beach, California, as well as other versions. See pp. 21–23.

Folklorist Gary Alan Fine suggests that this legend reflects anger over Mexican workers who entered the United States illegally and competed for jobs held by Americans. The Mexicans are represented by a pet that turns out to be a rat. He cites a similar legend in France based on the arrival of workers from Africa and the Near East. See Fine, pp. 158–59.

Maybe You Will Remember: How the Story Ends.

What happened to Rosemary's mother?

When the hotel doctor saw Mrs. Gibbs, he knew at once that she was about to die. She had a form of the plague, a dread disease that killed quickly and caused frightening epidemics.

If the word got out that a woman had died of the plague in the heart of Paris, there would be panic. People in the hotel and elsewhere would rush to escape. The doctor knew what the hotel's owners expected. He was to keep the case a secret. Otherwise, they would lose lots of money.

To get Rosemary out of the way, the doctor sent her to the other side of Paris for some worthless medicine. As he expected, Mrs. Gibbs died soon after she left. Her body was smuggled out of the hotel to a cemetery, where it was buried. A team of workmen quickly repainted the room and replaced everything in it.

The desk clerks were ordered to tell Rosemary that she was in the wrong hotel. When she insisted on seeing her room, it had become a different place, and, of course, her mother had vanished. All those involved were warned that they would lose their jobs if they gave away the secret.

To avoid panic in the city, the police and the newspapers agreed to say nothing of the death. No police reports were filed; no news stories appeared. It was as if Rosemary's mother and her room had never existed.

In another version of the story, Rosemary and her mother had separate rooms. Mrs. Gibbs died during the night while Rosemary was asleep. Her body was removed. Then her room was repainted and refurnished. When Rosemary could not find her mother the next morning, she was told that her mother was not with her when she checked in.

After many months of searching, a friend, a relative, or the young woman herself finds someone who works in the hotel and, for a bribe, reveals what happened.

This legend was the basis of a movie, *So Long at the Fair,* that appeared in 1950. The story also inspired two novels, one published as early as 1913. But the story was old even then. The writer Alexander Woollcott discovered that it had been reported as a true story in England in 1911 in the *London Daily Mail* and in America in 1889 in the *Detroit Free Press.* It became known throughout America and Europe. See Woollcott, pp. 87–94; Briggs and Tongue, p. 98; Burnham, pp. 94–95.

The Red Spot: There are several versions of this legend in America and Great Britain. Spiders actually lay their eggs in cocoons or egg sacs that they spin from silk and leave in secluded places. Folklorist Brunvand suggests that stories like these grow from a common fear of having our bodies invaded by such creatures. See Brunvand, *The Mexican Pet,* pp. 76–77.

No, Thanks: This story is based loosely on one reported in *The New York Times*, March 2, 1983, p. C2.

WHAT IS GOING ON HERE?

The Trouble: When no cause could be found for the strange events in this story, many people wondered if a noisy, mischief-making ghost called a poltergeist was responsible. Stories of poltergeist hauntings have been common in our folklore for centuries. It was said that these poltergeists caused objects to fly and furniture to dance, pulled sheets and blankets from beds, made rapping and groaning sounds and other mischief.

At a ranch in Cisco, Texas, in 1881, something or someone threw rocks, opened locked doors without a key, squeezed raw eggs through the cracks in a ceiling, and mewed like a cat. Everything and everyone was checked, just as they were in "The Trouble." Some of what happened could have been caused by a prankster. But there were no explanations for much of it, except that a poltergeist had been at work. See Lawson and Porter.

Parapsychologists, such as the two in our story, are concerned with mental powers humans may have that are not yet understood. Psychokinesis (PK) and extrasensory perception (ESP) are examples of these powers.

"The Trouble" is based on news reports in *The New York Times, Life* magazine, and other publications. For stories of poltergeists and information on poltergeist research, see Carrington and Fodor, Creighton, Haynes, Hole, and Rogo.

WHOOOOOOOO?

Strangers: This brief tale is told in America and Britain. There are many settings for the story, including a turnip field and a museum.

The Hog: Ghosts are said to appear in many forms: as animals—in our story, a hog; as balls of fire and other lights; as living humans; and as specters. Some ghosts, of course, remain invisible, making their presence known only by their actions and sounds.

The story of the woman who returns as a hog is adapted and expanded from a Canadian ghost story told on Prince Edward Island. See Creighton, p. 206.

Is Something Wrong?: This story is expanded from a summary of an Afro-American ghost tale in Jones, "The Ghosts of New York," p. 240. It is related to a hoax tale about an encounter with a horrible monster. In that story, the monster is an escaped murderous lunatic. When he catches up with the man who is fleeing, he cries, "Tag, you rascal!" See Schwartz, *Tomfoolery*, p. 93, p. 116.

It's Him!: This is a version of the "Man from the Gallows" family of tales. It is adapted from two tellings. One is from the Cumberland Gap region of Kentucky; see Roberts, pp. 32–33. The other is in the University of Pennsylvania folklore archive. It was collected from Etta Kilgore in Wise, Virginia, in 1940, by Emory L. Hamilton. See the note to the story "Just Delicious."

T-H-U-P-P-P-P-P-P-P!: This story is an expansion of a

joke young children tell.

You May Be the Next...: This parody of the famous "Hearse Song" is from the folklore collection at the University of Massachusetts. It was contributed by Susan Young of Chelmsford, Massachusetts, in 1972. For a variant of the traditional song and its background, see Schwartz, *Scary Stories to Tell in the Dark,* p. 39, pp. 94–95.

Bibliography

BOOKS

Books that may be of particular interest to young people are marked with an asterisk (*).

Briggs, Katharine M. *A Dictionary of British Folktales.* 4 vols. Bloomington, Ind.: Indiana University Press, 1967.

———, and Ruth L. Tongue. *Folktales of England.* Chicago: University of Chicago Press, 1965.

*Brunvand, Jan H. *The Mexican Pet: More New Urban Legends and Some Old Favorites.* New York: W. W. Norton & Company, Inc., 1986.

*———. *The Vanishing Hitchhiker: American Urban Legends and Their Meanings.* New York: W. W. Norton & Company, Inc., 1981.

Burnham, Tom. *More Misinformation.* New York: Lippincott & Crowell, Publishers, 1980.

Carrington, Hereward, and Nandor Fodor. *Haunted People: Story of the Poltergeist Down the Centuries.* New York: New American Library, Inc., 1951.

Collison-Morley, Lacy. *Greek and Roman Ghost Stories.* Oxford: B. H. Blackwell, 1912.

*Creighton, Helen. *Bluenose Ghosts.* Toronto: Ryerson Press, 1957.

Curtin, Jeremiah. *Tales of the Fairies and the Ghost World: Irish Folktales from Southwest Munster.* London: David Nutt, 1895.

Ellison, William H., ed. *The Life and Adventures of George Nidever.* Berkeley, Cal.: University of California Press, 1937.

Hare, Augustus. *The Story of My Life.* London: George Allen & Unwin Ltd. An abridgment of Vols. 4, 5, and 6, George Allen, 1900.

Haynes, Renee. *The Hidden Springs: An Enquiry into Extra-Sensory Perception,* rev. ed. Boston: Little, Brown and Company, 1973.

Hole, Christina. *Haunted England: A Survey of English Ghost-Lore.* London: P. T. Batsford Ltd., 1940.

*Johnson, Clifton. *What They Say in New England and Other American Folklore.* Boston: Lee and Shepherd, 1896. Reprint edition, Carl A. Withers, ed. New York: Columbia University Press, 1963.

*Jones, Louis C. *Things That go Bump in the Night.* New York: Hill and Wang, 1959.

*Kipling, Rudyard. *The Jungle Book.* New York: Harper and Brothers, 1893.

Lüthi, Max. *Once Upon a Time: On the Nature of Fairy Tales.* Bloomington, Ind.: Indiana University Press, 1976.

*O'Dell, Scott. *Island of the Blue Dolphins.* Boston: Houghton Mifflin Company, 1960.

Randolph, Vance. *Ozark Superstitions.* New York: Columbia University Press, 1947. Reprint edition, *Ozark Magic and Superstitions.* New York: Dover Publications, Inc., 1964.

Roberts, Leonard. *Old Greasybeard: Tales from the Cumberland Gap.* Detroit: Folklore Associates, 1969. Reprint edition, Pikesville, Ky.: Pikesville College Press, 1980.

Rogo, D. Scott. *The Poltergeist Experience.* Harmonds worth, England: Penguin Books Ltd., 1979.

*Schwartz, Alvin. *More Scary Stories to Tell in the Dark.*

New York: J. B. Lippincott, 1984.

*———. *Scary Stories to Tell in the Dark.* New York: J. B. Lippincott, 1981.

*———. *Telling Fortunes: Love Magic, Dream Signs, and Other Ways to Tell the Future.* New York: J. B. Lippincott, 1987.

*———. *Tomfoolery: Trickery and Foolery with Words.* Philadelphia: J. B. Lippincott Company, 1973.

Shattuck, Roger. *The Forbidden Experiment: The Story of the Wild Boy of Aveyron.* New York: Farrar, Straus & Giroux, Inc., 1980.

Shelley, Mary Wollstonecraft. *Frankenstein, or the Modern Prometheus.* Indianapolis: The Bobbs-Merrill Company, Inc., 1974.

Thompson, Stith. *The Folktale.* Berkeley, Cal.: University of California Press, 1977.

———, ed. *Folk Tales and Legends.* The Frank C. Brown Collection of North Carolina Folklore, Vol. 1. Durham, N. C.: Duke University Press, 1952.

Tongue, Ruth L. *Forgotten Folk-Tales of the English Counties.* London: Routledge & Kegan Paul Ltd., 1970.

Van Paassen, Pierre. *Days of Our Years.* New York: Hillman-Curl, Inc., 1939.

Widdowson, John. *If You Don't Be Good: Verbal Social Control In Newfoundland.* St. John's, Newfoundland: Memorial University of Newfoundland, 1977.

Woollcott, Alexander. *While Rome Burns.* New York: The Viking Press, Inc., 1934.

Yarborough, Willard, ed. *The Best Stories of Bert Vincent.* Knoxville, Tenn.: Brazos Press, 1968.

ARTICLES

Balfour, M. C. "Legends of the Lincolnshire Cars, Part 2." *Folklore* 2 (1891): 271–78.

Bertillion, L. D. "The Lobo Girl of Devil's River." *Straight Texas.* Publications of the Texas Folklore Society 13 (1937): 79–85.

Cox, John Harrington. "The Witch Bridle." *Southern Folklore Quarterly* 7 (1943): 203–9.

Fife, Austin E. "The Wild Girl of the Santa Barbara Channel Islands. *California Folklore Quarterly* 2 (1943): 149–50.

Fine, Gary Alan. "Mercantile Legends and the World Economy: Dangerous Imports from the Third World." *Western Folklore* 48 (1989): 153–62.

Graves, Robert. "Praise Me and I Will Whistle to You." *The New Republic,* Sept. 1, 1958, 10–15.

Jones, Louis C. "The Ghosts of New York: An Analytical Study." *Journal of American Folklore* 57 (1944): 237–54.

Lawson, O. G., and Kenneth W. Porter. "Texas Poltergeist, 1881." *Journal of American Folklore* 64 (1951): 371–82.

Lüthi, Max. "Parallel Themes in Folk Narrative and in Art Literature." *Journal of the Folklore Institute* 6 (1967): 3–16.

The New York Times. Articles in 1958 regarding incidents described in "The Trouble," a story in this book: issues of Feb. 3, 6, 7, 9, 20, 22, 24, 25, 27; Mar. 6, 26, 29.

———. "Stranger in the Night." Metropolitan Diary, Mar. 3, 1982, C2.

Parler, Mary Celestia. "The Wolf Boy." *Arkansas Folklore* 6 (1956): 4.

Wallace, Robert. "House of Flying Objects." *Life*, Mar. 17, 1958, 49–58. Regarding incidents in the story "The Trouble."

Ward, Donald. "The Return of the Dead Lover: Psychic Unity and Polygenesis Revisited." *Folklore on Two Continents: Essays in Honor of Linda Dégh*, 310–17. Eds.: Nikolai Burlakoff and Carl Lindahl. Bloomington, Ind.: Trickster Press, 1980.

Widdowson, John. "The Bogeyman: Some Preliminary Observations on Frightening Figures." *Folklore* 82 (1971): 90–115.

Acknowledgments

I thank the many boys and girls who asked for this third book of scary stories. I hope it pleases them. I also am grateful to the people who shared their stories with me and to the librarians and folklore archivists at the University of Maine at Orono, at the University of Pennsylvania, and at Princeton University for their help in my research. I thank Joseph Hickerson of the Library of Congress for identifying popular music based on the "vanishing hitchhiker" legend. And I am indebted as always to my wife and colleague Barbara Carmer Schwartz for her many contributions.

A.S.

ALVIN SCHWARTZ is known for a body of work of more than two dozen books of folklore for young readers that explore everything from wordplay and humor to tales and legends of all kinds. His collections of scary stories—SCARY STORIES TO TELL IN THE DARK, MORE SCARY STORIES TO TELL IN THE DARK, SCARY STORIES 3, and two I Can Read Books, IN A DARK, DARK ROOM and GHOSTS!—are just one part of his matchless folklore collection.

STEPHEN GAMMELL's drawings have appeared in a number of books for children, including SCARY STORIES TO TELL IN THE DARK, MORE SCARY STORIES TO TELL IN THE DARK, and SCARY STORIES 3. He is the winner of the Caldecott Medal for his drawings in SONG AND DANCE MAN by Karen Ackerman. His art in WHERE THE BUFFALOES BEGIN by Olaf Baker earned him a Caldecott Honor, the *Boston Globe–Horn Book* Award, and a *New York Times* Best Illustrated Book citation. He also won a Caldecott Honor for his art in THE RELATIVES CAME by Cynthia Rylant. Mr. Gammell lives in St. Paul, Minnesota.